Creatures

Here Comes a Candle. . .

Bear was there. He was four stairs from the top of the flight, and as Jess looked, he heaved himself clumsily up another step. He was very clumsy tonight because in one front paw, he was carrying a lit candle.

Jess couldn't stop herself. She gave a gasp that hissed sharply in the silence.

And Bear heard her.

In one rigid, terrified moment, Jess saw Bear lift his head and glare up to the landing. His beady eyes fixed on her face, and they seemed to glow with a ghastly light of their own. Their gazes locked, and Jess thought she saw Bear's mouth twist into a hideous leer.

**Look for other Creatures titles
by Louise Cooper:**

1 Once I Caught a Fish Alive
2 If You Go Down to the Woods
3 See How They Run
4 Who's Been Sitting in My Chair?
5 Atishoo! Atishoo! All Fall Down!
6 Give a Dog a Bone
7 Daddy's Gone A-Hunting
8 Incy Wincy Spider

Creatures at Christmas

Creatures

Here Comes a Candle. . .

Louise Cooper

Scholastic Children's Books
Commonwealth House, 1–19 New Oxford Street,
London WC1A 1NU, UK
London ~ New York ~ Toronto ~ Sydney ~ Auckland
Mexico City ~ New Delhi ~ Hong Kong

First published by Scholastic Ltd, 2000

Text copyright © Louise Cooper, 2000

ISBN 0 439 01339 9

All rights reserved
Typeset by Falcon Oast Graphic Art
Printed by Cox & Wyman Ltd, Reading, Berks

10 9 8 7 6 5 4 3 2 1

1

Spending the whole of Saturday morning at a car boot sale was definitely *not* Jessica's idea of a good time. And when it was the very first Saturday of the school summer holidays, and all her mates had gone swimming, that only made it worse.

"I don't see why I had to come," she complained to Mum, who was unpacking the car and spreading their stuff out on a mat. "Most of this is Dad's junk, anyway, so why couldn't he—"

"You know why – because he's got to work today," Mum interrupted. She stuck her head

1

and shoulders back inside the car and heaved at something large and heavy. "And most of this – (puff) – 'junk' is yours, not his; so if you want your share of the money, you can stop – (puff) – moaning and give me a hand!"

Jess sighed as she realized she wasn't going to get out of this. Grumpily, she grabbed a couple of small boxes, while Mum hauled out an enormous and truly hideous vase.

"Yeuch!" said Jess. "Isn't that the thing Nan gave you last Christmas?"

"Yes, and if you *ever* tell her, I'll murder you," Mum threatened. "I'm going to say it got broken." She stared at the vase as if it was something very dead and very nasty. "*Someone*'s got to like it."

"Nan'll probably go and buy you another one," said Jess.

"Oh, shut up and make yourself useful!"

Soon *everything* was spread out on the ground and they were ready for customers. But though the boot sale was busy, nobody seemed very interested in what Mum had to sell. A lot of people walked past, but after twenty minutes only three had bothered to stop, and none of them had *even* spent 20p.

Jess scowled at the rows of other cars and small vans in the field. She felt bored and sorry for herself. Right now, Emma and Jamie would be at the swimming pool, and there was a new wave machine there, and the café played good music, and. . .

Mum nudged her suddenly. "Jess! At least *try* and smile at people! Your long face is putting the customers off!"

"I don't feel like smiling," Jess retorted. "I'm fed up!"

Mum sighed exasperatedly. "Well, go and walk around for a bit. Go and do something. *Anything.*"

It was a better idea than sitting staring into space, so Jess went. She wandered up and down the rows of pitches, looking at what they had to offer. She had a few pounds of her allowance; she might find a CD or some books worth buying.

She didn't have any luck – until she came to the very last pitch in the second row.

It was a big pitch, and standing beside it was a boy of about Jess's age. He looked bored too, and they exchanged a sympathetic grin.

Then Jess stopped as she saw the mirror.

She'd been looking for one for ages, to put in her bedroom, and this was unusual – triangular, in a frame of a silvery metal with raised zigzag patterns. Jess thought it was absolutely great, and she looked at the boy again.

"Hi," he said.

"Hi," replied Jess. She nodded at the spread-out objects. "You've got a lot of things here."

The boy pulled a rueful face. "Tell me about it! It's all from my great-great-aunt's house. She died last month and left everything to my dad, so he's selling the stuff he doesn't want. This is only a bit of it – I reckon we'll be car-booting every week till Christmas!" He looked hopefully at her. "You interested in anything?"

"I might be," said Jess. "How much do you want for that mirror?"

"Oh, isn't there a price on it? I'd better find Mum and Dad. They've gone to the tea stall – can you hang on a minute?"

"Sure." The boy ran off, and while she waited, Jess took a closer look at the things his family were selling. It looked as if an antique shop had had a major clearout. Just about everything in the pitch was really old – delicate china, polished chairs, a big clock, ornaments. . . There was a whole box full of silver knives and forks that Mum would have killed for, and a huge, framed oil painting even more hideous than Nan's vase. Great-great-auntie-whoever must have been pretty eccentric, she thought.

Suddenly, the back of her neck prickled. Someone was watching her. She knew it; she could *feel* it, and quickly she turned round.

There was nobody behind her. But, from the top of a chest of drawers at the other end of the pitch, a pair of bright eyes stared beadily straight into her face.

Jess jumped – then laughed at herself as she saw the owner of the eyes. It was just a teddy-bear. It had been plonked on the chest of drawers and partly hidden behind a pile of books, so that only the top half of its head showed above them. Glad that no one else had seen her make a prat of herself, Jess walked over to where the bear sat.

"Stupid thing!" she said to it. "You gave me a fright!" She reached to pick it up and have a closer look at it – then suddenly stopped. She didn't want to touch the bear. She hadn't the foggiest idea why, but something about it made her skin crawl.

Jess frowned. She could see the bear more clearly now, and there was nothing weird about it. It was old, sure, but so what? So was everything else on the pitch. And OK, it was manky and one of its ears had flopped over. But otherwise, it was just an ordinary toy.

So why did it give her the creeps?

"Hi!" The voice behind her made her jump again, and she spun round to see that the boy had returned. A big, red-faced man – his dad, presumably – was with him, and he stared suspiciously at Jess.

"Glen says you're interested in the mirror."

"Um . . . yes. How much is it?"

"That's old, you know. Art Deco. I won't take less than ten for it."

"Ten pounds?" Jess's face fell. "I haven't got that much."

Glen's dad shrugged. "Sorry. Like I said, I won't take any less."

"Oh. Well, I'd better ask my mum, then." She *might* be persuaded, Jess thought, but it'd take some doing.

"OK," said Glen's dad, sounding as if he

couldn't care less. Then he paused. "I expect you can afford the bear, if you want it."

"What?" Jess was startled.

"The bear." He nodded towards the beady-eyed face. "I saw you looking at it."

"Dad—" Glen tried to interrupt, but his dad waved a "shut up" signal at him. "It's not worth much in that condition, so you can have it for a pound."

Jess stared at the bear. The bear stared back. It had a label tied round its neck, she saw now. Something was written on the label. She didn't want to know what it was.

"No," she said. A shiver went through her despite the warm sunshine. "No, thanks. I don't want it."

She didn't give the man time to say anything else, but turned and ran back towards Mum's car.

Mum said all right, she'd go and look at the mirror, but she wasn't promising anything. While she was away, Jess sold a pair of trainers that she'd grown out of, two CDs by a band who were in last year but deeply naff now, and several of Dad's books. She thought she might get rid of Nan's vase, too, but the woman dithered so much that her husband lost his temper and stomped off. Jess grinned as she watched the woman run after him and heard them start up a steaming row, then abruptly the grin faded as, beyond them, she saw Mum coming back.

Mum had bought something from Glen's dad. But it wasn't the mirror Jess had wanted.

It was the teddy-bear.

"Look what I found!" Mum looked as happy as a little kid with six ice-creams. "Isn't he brilliant?"

Jess stared at the bear. The bear stared at Jess. It wasn't possible – of course it wasn't – but it seemed to have a smirk on its face.

"Mum," she said in a small voice, "what about the mirror?"

"Oh, that. Sorry, Jess, but it's much too expensive for what it is! That man's really greedy; he wants stupid prices for most of the stuff he's got."

"Oh." Jess's voice was even smaller.

Mum was too pleased with herself to notice. She turned the bear around, looking at him from every angle, and said, "Do you know, I think he might be nearly a hundred years old! What a find – and that man obviously didn't know, or he'd have charged *much* more than a pound!" She brushed some dust off the bear's patchy fur. "The label will probably tell us something. I didn't look at it at the pitch. Let's see, now. . ."

She peered at the label for a few moments. Then she frowned.

"Oh. I thought it'd have the maker's name or something, but it hasn't. It's a rhyme. Look."

She held the bear out to Jess, and it was all Jess could do to stop herself from flinching backwards. Without touching the bear (she *still* didn't want to), she looked at the label.

It was strange, crabby writing and it was very faded. But the words were still readable. They said:

> *My name is Bear,*
> *I sit and stare*
> *And when I'm there*
> *You should not dare.*
> *So have a care –*
> *O friend, beware!*

Jess swallowed, hard. "Wh-what does *that* mean?" she whispered.

"I've no idea." Then Mum's expression cleared. "Probably some children wrote it – his owners, years ago. I expect it was for a game they were playing, and it never got taken off." She smiled. "It's rather sweet, isn't it? Sort of part of his history. I'll leave it on him. And at least we know his name now."

Yeah, thought Jess. *We do, don't we? And I wish we didn't.*

2

"Phooh!" Mum said as they arrived home. "Bonfire Bill's at it again!"

There was a cloud of smoke drifting over their house from the next-door garden, and they could see their neighbour putting more garden rubbish on it. "Bonfire Bill", as Dad had nicknamed him, was a real pest in the summer. He had bonfires in his garden almost every day, and no amount of complaining could persuade him to stop.

Mum glared over the fence as she got out of the car, but Bonfire Bill only grinned and waved cheerily. Mum muttered under her breath, but Jess took no notice. She had other things to worry about. Her neck had been prickling all the way home. She'd been horribly aware of Bear in the back of the car with the stuff they hadn't sold (including Nan's vase), and couldn't shake off the feeling of those awful, beady-bright eyes boring into her. A couple of times she'd turned round quickly, half convinced that she'd catch Bear creeping up on her. She hadn't, of course. But her whole day had been unpleasantly and absolutely ruined.

By the time Dad came back from his job at the town's biggest store, Bear was installed in the sitting-room alcove where Mum displayed all her favourite treasures. Mum loved collecting strange objects, and Bear looked strangest of all as he stared out at his new surroundings. He kept on staring at Jess, too, until she could hardly stand being in the same room with him.

She hoped that Dad would take one look at Bear and say, "I'm not having that thing in here!" But to her dismay, Dad liked Bear as much as Mum did. He said Bear reminded him of his grandad's old teddy, and he picked him up and stroked him and smoothed his fur, and went on about making him a special shelf all of his own. Behind Mum and Dad's backs Jess pulled a hideous face at Bear and made a rude gesture. Bear just went on staring at her, as if he couldn't have cared less.

Jess didn't sleep well that night. All her dreams were about beady eyes following her wherever she went, and she tossed and turned restlessly until morning. When she got up, it was raining (why did it always rain at the start of the summer holidays?), and she did *not* want to spend any time in the sitting-room. So she stayed in her bedroom until lunch was ready.

Over lunch, Mum said, "We're going over to Uncle Paul's this afternoon, Jess. Do you want to come?"

Uncle Paul was just about the most boring human being ever born, so Jess shook her head quickly. "No, thanks." An idea came to her, and hopefully she added, "Can I ask Emma and Jamie over?"

"Well . . . I suppose so," said Mum, who was never too keen on letting Jess and her friends loose in the house on their own. "If you promise to behave yourselves."

Jess thought that was pretty dumb. If they

weren't going to behave, she'd hardly let on to Mum, would she? But she only said, "Thanks," and tried to look innocent. She just hoped Emma and Jamie hadn't already fixed up something else.

To her relief, they hadn't, and they both arrived just before Mum and Dad left, in time to get the standard lecture about not making a mess, or playing loud music and annoying the neighbours. Emma was Jess's best friend, and Jamie a pretty close second, and they could always be relied on to come up with fun ideas.

"OK," Jamie said, as Mum and Dad drove away and the three of them stood in the hall. "Let's find something to do. If we go in the sitting-room—"

"No," said Jess quickly.

Her friends both looked puzzled. "Why ever not?" Emma asked.

"Because. . ." Oh, this was crazy. She'd either have to pretend there was nothing wrong, or tell them the truth. If she told, they'd laugh at her.

"Nothing," she said. "Go on, then."

They trooped in. Jamie glanced at the alcove – and stopped.

"What on earth's *that*?" he demanded, pointing at Bear.

Jess sighed. "Mum got him yesterday, at the car boot sale. I *hate* him."

"Don't blame you!" Jamie walked towards the alcove, Emma at his heels. "What a cruddy, manky old thing! Where'd he come from – the Ark?"

Jess shrugged, looking at the floor so that she didn't have to meet Bear's blank stare. "Someone was selling off a load of junk from an old relation."

"Selling it?" Emma echoed. "They should have chucked it in the nearest skip!"

"Some of it was all right," said Jess. "There was this mirror that I—" She stopped. As she spoke she had looked up, and saw to her horror that Emma had taken Bear down from the shelf and was turning him over in her hands.

"Put him back!" she said agitatedly. She didn't know why, but she didn't want either of them to touch Bear. The idea of it *scared* her.

"Stop getting your knickers in a twist!" Emma grinned at her. "Your mum's not here, so she won't know!"

15

"It isn't that, it's. . ." But Jess stopped again as she realized that what she wanted to say would sound totally stupid. Anyway, Emma wasn't listening. She'd seen Bear's label now, and she was reading it.

". . . 'So have a care – O friend, beware' . . ." she quoted. "What's *that* supposed to mean?"

"Let's see." Jamie grabbed Bear from her and turned him upside-down to look at the dangling label. "Hey, weird! Did your mum do that, Jess?"

"Of course she didn't!" Jess snapped. "She isn't *that* cretinous; she. . ." The words tailed off as she realized that her friends were both giving her funny looks.

Then: "OK, OK," said Emma soothingly. "What's got into you today?"

"Nothing!"

"She's lying," Jamie told Emma.

"Yeah, she is. Come on, Jess, what's going on? We're your friends. You can tell us."

They *were* her friends, weren't they? Jess thought. So if she told them about the creepy feelings Bear had given her, they'd understand and they wouldn't laugh.

"Well," she said, "It's like this. . ."

Emma and Jamie listened. And when Jess had finished, they both burst out laughing.

"That's *brill*!" Jamie spluttered. "A haunted teddy-bear – honest, Jess, you really come up with the most idiotic things!"

"I didn't say he's haunted!" Jess protested. "But there *is* something creepy about him. And that rhyme—"

"Was done by someone who wanted to put the wind up someone else!" Emma interrupted, between giggles. "Oo-oo-ooh, Jess!" She hunched her shoulders and waggled clawed hands above her head, putting on a spooky voice. "Ghoulies and ghosties and long-leggedy beasties. . ."

"And bears that go bump in the night!" Jamie added, and showed his teeth like Count Dracula. "Look out, Jess, there's something creeping up *behiiiind* you!"

"Oh, shut up!" Jess was almost in tears of embarrassment and fury. "Stop winding me up, the pair of you! You're mean!"

Emma looked offended. "Oh come on, it's only a joke! What's the matter with you? Look." She snatched Bear back from Jamie and thrust him towards Jess, who jumped back as if he was a poisonous snake. "There's nothing spooky about him," Emma insisted. "He's just a tatty old toy that your mum was brainless enough to spend money on, right?" She waved one of Bear's arms and went into another comic voice. "Hell-ooo, Jess! I'm Brainless Bear, with my stupid stare, and I don't care, so there!"

"Hey, give him here." Jamie's eyes had lit up with mischief. "Look – if you twist his legs backwards, his feet turn in and he does silly walks. Like this." He marched Bear across the back of the sofa. "I'm coming to get yooou!" he hooted.

Emma gleefully joined in the fun, and the two of them got to work. They bent Bear into every ludicrous position they could think of, tangling his legs, folding his ears over his face, doubling him up backwards. Jess watched with growing horror, until suddenly she couldn't stand it any more.

"Stop it!" she yelled. "Just *stop* it, will you!"

They stopped, and stared at her. Jess's face was crimson and her eyes were filling with tears. Emma and Jamie looked uncomfortably at each other, then Emma bit her lip. "It was only a joke," she said, sounding a bit ashamed.

"Well, the joke's over!"

"All right, all right." From the corner of her eye Emma saw that Jamie was still twisting Bear around, and she added, "Leave it, Jamie. Put the thing down."

Jamie shrugged, and dropped Bear on the sofa, where he lay with one leg sticking up, staring at the ceiling.

"Put him back," said Jess in a shaky voice.

Jamie didn't feel like taking orders. "Put him back yourself, if you're that bothered," he said grouchily. "He's your bear."

"He isn't!"

"Oh, I'll do it!" Emma snatched Bear up and shoved him any old how on the shelf again. "There! Satisfied?" She put her fists on her hips and looked round the room. "Well, that *was* fun, wasn't it?" she went on sarcastically. "What can we do that's even more exciting? Play I-Spy?"

Jess said nothing, and Jamie looked out of the window. "It's stopped raining," he said. "You two can do what you want, but I'm going to walk up to town."

"Me too," Emma agreed. She paused, looking at Jess. "Coming?"

Jess nodded. She wanted to get out of the house, and wouldn't have cared if there'd been a thunderstorm, a hurricane *and* an earthquake crashing outside. "Yeah," she said. "Anything's got to be better than hanging around here."

She was last out of the sitting-room, and at the door she turned and glanced uneasily back towards the alcove. Bear looked very undignified where Emma had stuck him. Mum wouldn't be pleased; she'd know they'd been messing around, and Jess would get it in the neck. She ought to move him to the position he'd been in before. . .

Then she saw Bear's eyes. Just for a moment, they didn't look like glass. There was an awful kind of *life* in them, and they seemed to fix her with glowering hatred. A look that said: *I'll get my own back – you wait and see.*

Jess swallowed. Then she turned and ran after Emma and Jamie.

3

"Oo-*owww*!" Emma hopped and stumbled again, and nearly tipped Jess completely off balance. "I've broken it, I *know* I have! Ooh, it *hurts*!"

Jamie grabbed her from the other side, pulling her upright again, and the three of them stopped for breath. Jess's shoulder was going numb where Emma leaned on it, and she thought that at this rate it'd be Wednesday before they got home.

"You should have looked where you were going instead of staring into space," she said crossly. "Falling off the edge of the kerb – how can you be so dumb?"

"I didn't *see* it," said Emma miserably. "Oww! Honest, I *have* broken my ankle!"

"No, you haven't." Jamie was no more sympathetic than Jess. "It's twisted, that's all. Stick a bag of frozen peas on it and it'll be fine."

"I don't carry bags of frozen peas around with me!" Emma snapped. She was angry because the accident had been so stupid. Ninety-nine times out of a hundred she could have done the same thing and not hurt herself at all. But this had been hundredth-time bad luck.

"Come on." Jamie was getting bored and impatient. "If we go to the shopping centre we might get a bus to Emma's place. Let's cross the road."

They walked/hopped to the nearest junction. The traffic lights were red, and there were no cars waiting. As they prepared to cross, Jamie said, "I'm starting to think I'm the only one around here with half a gramme of sense! First Jess going loopy about that grotty old bear, and now Emma floating around with her brain disconnected." He started to step off the pavement. "I don't know why I even bother to—"

"*Jamie!*" Jess shouted. "*Look out!*"

Jamie saw the car only just in time. With a yell he sprang back on to the pavement, and the car shot past exactly where he would have been if he'd taken another step. A bow-wave of water sprayed up and soaked their legs, and they all stood staring wide-eyed as the vehicle went on its way.

"The lights have turned green," Emma said in a small voice.

"Yeah. . ." Jamie sounded very shaky. "I didn't see. I forgot to look again." He let out his breath with a huff. "Thanks, Jess. Thanks a million."

Jess said nothing. Her heart was pounding and she felt sick. One more step and Jamie could have been badly hurt. Even *killed.* Where had that car come from? They hadn't even *heard* it.

"I want to go home!" Emma insisted, "Before anything else happens."

"Yeah. Yeah, right." Jamie stared at the lights, and this time they were all very careful to wait until they'd turned red, and the traffic had stopped, before starting across. There was a bus at the shopping centre stop, and they climbed aboard and sat in silence all the way to Emma's house. Emma didn't ask them in but hopped miserably indoors, and Jamie didn't want to go back to Jess's. Instead he said he'd see them both tomorrow, probably, and went.

Mum and Dad were back by the time Jess got home, and Mum was none too pleased when she saw Bear.

"If Emma and Jamie wanted to look at him, why couldn't they put him back properly?" she grumbled. "It's not asking *too* much to tidy up after yourselves, is it?" She picked Bear up and smoothed his fur, almost stroking it. "Poor Bear; were they messing around with you? And while we're on the subject of being tidy, Jess, I've got better things to do than run round clearing up the mess you leave in the kitchen! When I was your age. . ."

She gave Jess the familiar lecture, at the same time placing Bear carefully back in his proper place on the alcove shelf. Jess had to force herself to look at Bear's eyes. They no longer had that scarily lifelike glint, but there was still something about his expression that made her nervous. Bear looked . . . smug? Yes, she decided; that was the word. Smug. As if he knew something she didn't. Something she'd find out about soon.

Something she wouldn't like *at all*.

It was several days before Jess began to realize what was going on; and when she did, she tried everything to stop herself believing it.

Emma's ankle had been the first thing. She wasn't badly injured – as Jamie had said, it was only a twist – but it hurt, and she would be limping for a while. Then, the same evening, she broke her personal stereo. She rang Jess to moan about it. "I wasn't *really* being careless, but I was thinking about my ankle, and the stereo was on the floor, and I couldn't *help* treading on it. . ." Her parents had told her it was her own fault, and no, they wouldn't buy her a new one; she'd have to save up for it. "*And* I stubbed the toes on my other foot in the kitchen," Emma finished tragically. "It's not fair!"

Then there was Jamie. It was Thursday before Jess found out what had happened to him. Like Emma, he had had a series of little mishaps. Nothing serious, but it added up to a badly bruised knee and elbow from falling off his skateboard, the complete disappearance of his favourite pair of trainers, and two broken dinner plates that had got him in trouble with his Mum.

Jess made sympathetic noises when he told her about it, and that afternoon she went to see how Emma was getting on.

Emma was still feeling miserable. Her ankle was getting better, but it seemed that she couldn't do a single thing right at the moment. She'd stubbed her toe again, couldn't find her school holiday project anywhere (she must have left it in class at the end of term), and her dad had found out that she'd been to see a film she wasn't supposed to, so she was in trouble.

She was feeling dramatic, too. "Remember that movie where they find this weird object washed up on a beach?" she asked. "Then everything starts going wrong, and it turns out that this thing's got a curse on it, so everyone who touches it gets jinxed. Well, I think it's happened to me!"

"Don't be daft," said Jess. "You haven't found any weird objects. Anyway, Jamie keeps having silly accidents too, so it isn't just you."

"Well, why's it happening then?" Emma persisted.

"How should I know? Maybe the Moon's in Taurus, or something. Or . . ." Jess stopped.

"What?" Emma prompted.

"Nothing." But a cold, clammy feeling had clutched at Jess's stomach. *A weird object with a curse on it*. . . No. It couldn't be that.

She didn't say anything to Emma. Instead, she stayed until she was tired of hearing the self-pitying stories, then went home. For reasons that she didn't want to admit to herself, she was *extremely* careful every time she had to cross a road. When she got home – in one piece – she went to the sitting-room and looked at Bear sitting on his shelf.

"It can't be!" she said, aloud but very quietly. "It just *can't*."

Bear looked back at her. The light from the window made his beady eyes shine very brightly, and Jess could have sworn that he was smiling.

Slowly, cautiously, she walked up to him

27

and, without touching, looked at the label around his neck.

> *And when I'm there*
> *You should not dare.*
> *So have a care –*
> *O friend, beware!*

A shiver went through her and she looked at Bear's face again.

"You haven't?" she whispered. "Have you. . .?"

Bear, of course, couldn't and didn't answer. But he still seemed to smile.

Jess shivered again, and went upstairs.

In her room, she sat on the bed and thought very hard indeed. As Nan would have put it, Emma had slobbered a bibful of truth when she'd said what she did about a jinx. There wasn't any evidence; at least, not yet. But the coincidence was more than a bit weird. First Emma, then Jamie – and it had all started after they'd messed around with Bear. Add the ominous warning in the rhyme, and it began to look scary.

And if Emma and Jamie had already been hit by the jinx, how long would it be before she, Jess, was affected too?

Jess looked uneasily around, and started to imagine all the accidents that could happen to her. Even in here there were loads of possibilities: she could break things, trip over things, fall out of bed, fall out of the window and be smashed to bits on the ground—

"Oh, stop it!" she told herself angrily. This was insane – she was working herself up to a state where she'd *make* accidents happen! Nothing really awful had become of Emma or Jamie, so even if Bear *did* have something to do with it (which he didn't, Jess added firmly), it wasn't anything to be frightened of. Another day or two and the silly mishaps would stop, and then she'd be laughing at the whole crazy notion.

Nothing bad happened to Jess that day, and by bedtime she was feeling better. Emma had said that she'd probably come over tomorrow morning, ankle or no ankle, so Jess went to sleep making plans for what they might do.

She had a dream in which her class teacher

turned into a giraffe and started speaking French. The dream was so daft that it woke her, and she lay blinking in the dark, surprised to find the giraffe gone. *Crazy!* she thought. Whatever time was it? She didn't know, but there were no sounds from downstairs and the street lights had gone out, so it must be pretty late.

She turned over and settled herself to go back to sleep. Then:

Thub. It was only a small noise, but she was sure she hadn't imagined it. And it came from directly below her.

Thub. There it was again. *What on earth. . . ?* Jess thought, and sat up, listening harder.

Thub. It sounded like something hitting something else, but gently – a bit like a tennis ball bouncing on a carpet. It *did* come from below, and Jess's nerves started to tingle as she remembered which room was right underneath hers. The sitting-room. Where Bear was. . .

Nah. There had to be a perfectly rational explanation. It was probably something in the house – water pipes or whatever – and it happened *every* night, only she wasn't usually awake to hear it.

Thub. She jumped, and her pulse raced. Oh, this was stupid! She was getting the wind up over nothing at all, and that annoyed her. With an irritable sigh Jess got out of bed, stomped to the door, opened it and looked out.

The landing was dark, but there was a glimmer of light on the staircase. The banisters cast tall, thin shadows that looked spooky and menacing. But that was all. There was nothing out there. And the noise had stopped now.

Crossly, Jess closed her door and went back to bed.

She was asleep when the soft *thubs* began again. She didn't wake up. Not even when the noises became a *little* bit louder.

And more than a *little* bit closer. . .

4

Jess had an accident the next morning. As she tore downstairs in her usual rush, her elbow knocked Nan's vase, which was back on its stand in the hall. (You never knew when Nan might call round.) The vase rocked, teetered . . . then keeled over and shattered on the floor. Mum and Dad came running, and Jess expected to be bawled out for being so clumsy. But Dad started to laugh, then Mum joined in, and they both said it was a brilliant solution to the problem.Still grinning, Dad put the broken bits in the dustbin, and the horrified feeling that had struck Jess faded away.

She did wonder for a little while if the vase's destruction was the first sign of a jinx, but she soon decided that it wasn't. Her parents were pleased to have got rid of the hideous object, so surely it was a good thing? That cheered her up, and she decided, once and for all, to stop worrying.

There was an item on the local news that morning about a bus and a car that had collided in the town high street. No one was hurt and there wasn't much damage, but it had caused an gigantic traffic-jam. Jess only half listened, and didn't think anything more about it.

Until lunchtime.

Emma hadn't turned up as she'd said she would, so at last Jess phoned her. Emma was at home – and as soon as she heard Jess's voice, she started to babble.

"It was awful, Jess, it was really awful! I mean, the car just sort of skewed round and came sliding towards us, and there wasn't a thing anyone could do, and the people at the front all screamed because they thought—"

"Hang on, hang on!" Jess interrupted. "What are you talking about?"

"The bus! This morning! I was taking my library books back!"

"*What?* You mean you were—"

"On it! Yes! I just *said*!"

As a matter of fact she hadn't, but then Emma often told her stories back to front. Jess's heart crashed into her shoes and she said hollowly, "Oh, God. . ."

"No one was hurt or anything," Emma went on breathlessly. "It was only a bump, really. But it scared the *life* out of me!"

It was scaring the life out of Jess, too. She was in the hall, and the sitting-room door was open, and she could see Bear on his shelf. She told herself she had to be imagining it, but she thought he looked pleased.

"Jess. . ." Emma said in a small voice.

"Uh?" Jess hadn't been listening. "What?"

"Could you come over?"

"Well. . . yes, I suppose. But I thought you wanted to come here." Emma had a noisy baby sister and liked to get away from her as often as possible.

"I . . . don't feel like going out," Emma admitted. "And there's something I want to talk you about. Without. . ." She paused.

34

"Without your mum around."

She'd been going to say something different, Jess knew it. But she'd changed her mind at the last moment, and Jess had a horrible feeling she knew why.

"OK," she said. "I've got to have lunch first, though. I'll be there about half-past two."

"Thanks." Emma sounded relieved. "And on the way. . ."

"What?"

"Be careful . . . yeah?"

Jess felt icy cold as she put the phone down.

Emma's baby sister was having a screaming tantrum when Jess arrived, so the two girls escaped to the garden. Behind the shed, where no one could see them, Jess took one look at Emma's face and decided to jump in at the deep end.

"I know what you want to talk to me about," she said. "It's Bear, isn't it?"

Emma nodded miserably. "I know it sounds stupid," she said, "but I've been thinking about what you said. Jamie and I laughed at you. Now, though. . ."

"You think he's jinxed."

Emma nodded. "Yeah. And Jamie and I've caught it, because we messed around with him and did all those stupid things. I'm *scared*, Jess. I really am!"

She wanted Jess to tell her that it wasn't true, and Bear was completely harmless. Jess couldn't, because she didn't believe it herself. But one thing didn't fit.

"If he *does* bring bad luck," she said, "then why haven't I been having accidents, too? Or Mum and Dad, for that matter?"

"I thought about that," Emma told her. "And I've got a theory. I reckon he only jinxes people who don't like him, or are nasty to him. We called him names and said he was manky, so that's why he's got it in for us."

"But I did that, too." Then suddenly Jess remembered something. Yes, all three of them had called Bear names. But there was one thing Emma and Jamie had done, that she hadn't.

They had *touched* him.

Could that be the secret? Did Bear's malevolent influence only work on people who had actually put their hands on him? It was a pretty far-fetched idea, but no more far-fetched than the thought that he could jinx anyone in the first place. If one was possible, the other was just as likely.

She told Emma what she was thinking, and Emma's eyes widened. "Oh, Jess!" she said. "You've got to make sure you *don't* touch him, not *ever*!"

Jess very definitely agreed with that. "But what are we going to do about you two?" she asked. "D'you think we ought to ring Jamie and warn him?"

Emma sighed. "Trouble is, he won't believe us. You know what Jamie's like: if he can't see it or hear it or eat it, it doesn't exist. He'd just laugh."

That was true. "All the same, we should keep an eye on him," Jess urged, "till we can find a way to make these accidents stop."

Emma gave her an uneasy look. "Fine," she said. "But how are we *going* to find a way? That's what I want to know."

And neither of them had an answer.

By the time she went home, Jess was feeling as jumpy as a kangaroo. She and Emma had tried to come up with some ideas, but their talk just

37

went round and round in circles and got nowhere. They'd wanted to ring Jamie but neither of them had dared, in case they found out that something else had happened to him. That, they both agreed, would just about be the final straw.

Bear was sitting in the alcove as usual, only now there were two candlesticks, with fancy candles, on either side of him. Mum had put them there, of course, because "he looked a bit sad, so I thought they'd cheer him up". Bear looked positively smug, Jess thought. And that gave her a new idea.

She waited until Mum was out of the room, then went up to the shelf and stood in front of Bear.

"Look," she said, trying to keep her voice steady, "if you're cross with me, then I'm sorry. I didn't mean to call you all the things I said." *Oh, didn't I? (Shut up, Jess! Don't even THINK that!)* "And Emma and Jamie didn't mean them, either. So if you *are* making these accidents happen, Bear. . ." (A quick glance over her shoulder: if Mum came back and found her talking to Bear, she'd never live it down!) "Then please stop. *Please!*"

Bear stared back at her. He didn't look quite so smug now. Instead, there was a glint of triumph in his bright eyes. A very *nasty* glint.

Jess backed away. At the door she said one more "Please!" and then went up to her room. Well, she'd tried. What else could she do?

She only wished she believed it would work.

As Jess had feared, it didn't work. In fact, if anything, matters only got worse. Now it seemed that Emma and Jamie could hardly turn round without yet another thing going wrong, and by the following Tuesday Emma was nearly in hysterics when she rang Jess to tell her about the latest incidents.

Jess only had two consolations. First, the accidents were still very small ones that didn't do any real harm. And second, she still seemed to be immune. That didn't help Emma, of course; and as for Jamie – well, he didn't even know what was going on, because they couldn't pluck up the courage to tell him.

Then, on Wednesday afternoon, the thing Jess had dreaded most of all happened.

She'd been up to town and treated herself to a burger and milkshake lunch, and when she got back Mum said Emma had phoned.

"She asked if you could go round there," Mum said. "She sounded a bit funny on the phone, as if she'd been crying. What's it about, do you know?"

You bet I do! Jess thought, and shook her head. "No idea. I expect I'll find out, though. Is it OK if I go?"

"Yes, all right; but don't be late back. Oh, but first I want you to come and help me with something. It'll only take a minute."

Unsuspecting, Jess followed her into the sitting-room.

"Dad's going to put up that special shelf for Bear," Mum said. "He gets a bit lost in the alcove, among all the other things." She walked to where Bear was sitting. "But I'm not quite sure where's the best place, so what I want you to do is try a few different places, while I stand back and see what they look like."

She was taking Bear down from the shelf as she talked, and suddenly she turned round and thrust him at Jess. It was so unexpected that Jess didn't have time to think. Automatically, she reached out – and before she could do anything to stop it, Mum had plonked Bear straight into her hands.

For one single second Jess stared at Bear in utter horror. Then, with a yelp, she dropped him as if he'd been red hot.

"Jess, what on earth—" Mum began.

Jess wasn't listening. She wasn't even there any more. She had run out of the room, and was heading for the front door.

There was smoke rising behind the house. Bonfire Bill was at it again next door, but Jess didn't even notice. She ran half-way to the corner of the street before she could make herself stop. Then she leaned against a hedge, gasping until she got her breath back.

How could she have been so *stupid*? One careless moment, just one, and she'd fallen straight into the trap that was waiting for her! She'd touched Bear – and now, if she and Emma were right, she too would be jinxed.

She raised her head, feeling queasy. She couldn't go back to the house yet. Mum would demand an explanation, and she wouldn't know what to say. She'd better go to Emma's first, and maybe between them they could think up a story for her to use.

41

She walked shakily on, too dazed to hear what was coming towards her from the next street.

It was a kid, going full-pelt on a bike. He reached the corner at the same moment as Jess, and they collided and crashed to the ground in a tangle of arms, legs and spinning wheels.

"*Ohh!* You stupid little moron, why don't you look where you're going?" Jess shrieked. The kid jumped to his feet, grabbed his bike and aimed a kick at her.

"Drop dead, tomato-face!" He jumped on the bike, pulled a hideous face at her and ped-alled off again at top speed, leaving Jess sprawled on the pavement.

She picked herself up. There was a long graze down her left leg and her shoulder hurt where she'd fallen on it. But the kid had got away without a scratch, and so had his bike.

She watched the little brat until he was out of sight, and even when he'd vanished she went on staring at the spot where he'd disappeared. Her face was grim, because there was no doubt in her mind that this wasn't a coincidence. No doubt at all.

Bear's jinx had latched on to her, too.

And this was just the beginning.

5

By Friday, Jess's hopes of escaping the jinx had well and truly gone.

She had become every bit as accident-prone as Emma and Jamie. They were all little mishaps, but there were so many of them that it couldn't possibly be coincidence. Bumps, bruises, tripping over, breaking objects – even Dad, who didn't usually notice things like that, remarked that Jess seemed very clumsy all of a sudden.

And all the time Bear stared down from his shelf, looking thoroughly pleased with himself.

On Friday afternoon, the three friends met

at Emma's house. Jess and Emma were tense and snappy, but Jamie was very quiet; in fact they could hardly get a word out of him.

Until Emma said suddenly, "It's no use, Jess. We've got to tell him."

Jamie's head came up sharply. "Tell me what?" he demanded.

Jess bit her lip and Emma said, "It's about these accidents we all keep having. Jess and I – we've got this idea. . ."

"It's only a theory," said Jess uneasily. Then she saw that Jamie was uneasy as well. In fact, he looked dead nervous.

Suddenly he said, "I've been thinking, too. You're going to laugh, but. . ." His voice trailed off.

"But?" Emma prompted.

Jamie shrugged. "Nah, it's stupid. Forget it."

Jess narrowed her eyes at him. "What if we said the word 'jinx'?"

Jamie jumped visibly, and she knew at once that she'd hit the target. She heaved an enormous sigh of relief and went on, "OK. Come on, Em. Let's tell him everything."

They did – and, as Jess had suspected, Jamie's suspicions about the accidents followed exactly the same pattern as theirs. The only thing he hadn't thought of was the link with Bear.

"Oh, come on!" he said. "You can't really believe *that*! I mean, it's just a grotty old toy!"

"Sure," said Jess. "But you and Em touched him, and that's when your bad luck started. Then on Wednesday afternoon I touched him, too. And guess what? Suddenly I'm unlucky, just like you!"

"Yeah, but. . ." Jamie blinked. "It's a *toy*, Jess! It isn't *alive*!"

"What about that label round his neck?" Emma reminded him darkly. "That creepy rhyme – like a warning."

"'O friend, beware',," Jess quoted. "Whoever wrote that *knew* something."

"OK, OK!" Jamie held up both hands. "Say you're right. Say it *is* something to do with the bear. Then we know what to do, don't we? Just start being nice to it, and the bad luck'll stop."

Jess shook her head. "I've already tried that. It didn't work."

"All right; then get rid of it! Throw it out, or give it to some little kid – your mum'll go berserk, but it's worth it."

45

Emma groaned, and rolled her eyes. "He doesn't get it, does he?" she said to Jess. "He thinks it's going to be *easy!*"

Patiently, they explained to Jamie that simply getting rid of Bear was *not* a good idea. They didn't know what he was capable of, so how could they be sure he wouldn't get his revenge? The situation was bad enough already; if they dumped Bear, it might get a lot worse.

"That's crazy," Jamie said. "If Bear's not around, he can't do anything, can he?" He stood up and walked moodily towards the window. "Jess is just scared because of her mum. I say we should – oooh – *waah!*"

The girls goggled as, with a shout, Jamie went crashing to the floor. He sat up, looking baffled and shocked, and they ran to help him to his feet.

"Jamie!"

"Are you OK?"

"What happened?"

Then Jess saw the plastic truck. It was a baby's toy, with a garish yellow body and red wheels. It had trundled across the floor and come to rest against an armchair a metre from where Jamie sprawled. And it was exactly the right size for a foot to tread on.

Jamie wasn't hurt, luckily. But he'd changed his mind about getting rid of Bear.

"So what *are* we going to do?" Emma asked as the three of them sat down again and Jamie rubbed his bashed knee.

Jamie muttered and mumbled but didn't have any ideas. Jess, though, was thinking back to the car boot sale. What was the name of that boy at the pitch where Mum had bought Bear? Glen, that was it; she'd heard his dad say so. Glen had grumbled that the stuff they were selling came from his great-great-aunt's house and they'd be car-booting for ages before they got rid of it all. There was a sale every Saturday. Glen and his parents would surely be there tomorrow, and he *knew* something about Bear. Jess would have bet her life on it.

So maybe they should find out what it was.

She put the idea to Emma and Jamie, and they agreed that it made sense.

"So long as we can get there in one piece," Jamie added gloomily.

"Oh, shut up!" said Emma. "We can't lurk

indoors for ever because we're too scared to go out! We'll be careful, that's all."

"*Very* careful," Jess added.

Emma nodded. "Right, then. We'll meet up at Jess's house. There's a bus at ten o'clock that goes past the car boot site, isn't there, Jess? Great. And we'd better all think about what we're going to say to this Glen." She looked at them both in turn. "I mean, it's not exactly going to be easy, is it? He might not want to listen."

"He'll have to," Jess said grimly. She was starting to feel angry – and that, she thought, was a good sign. "I don't care what it takes. I'll make him listen, if it's the last thing I do!"

Jess was feeling much happier by the time she got home. But the feeling didn't last for long.

She didn't have any more accidents. It was just that when she went into the sitting-room (she couldn't avoid it completely, or her parents would have noticed), Bear had a look on his face that she'd never seen before. It was a thoughtful look, and a very menacing one. As if Bear was pondering very hard about something. *Planning* something.

As if, Jess told herself nervously, he knew exactly what had been going on at Emma's house, and wasn't pleased about it.

She went to her room straight after dinner, got into bed and read a magazine, which seemed the safest thing to do. At last she went to sleep, and if there were any more strange noises in the house at dead of night, they didn't disturb her.

Emma and Jamie arrived early the next morning, and they all caught the bus to the car boot sale field. There had been another string of little incidents, but no one felt like talking about them. They reached the sale without any more trouble, and started looking for Glen and his family.

"There they are!" Jess pointed to the far end of the field. "The blue estate car."

Glen's dad was talking to a customer, obviously trying to sell something. Glen stood by himself. He looked bored.

"Hi," said Jess casually as they walked up to him. "Remember me? Two weeks ago?"

His face brightened. "Yeah! You wanted that mirror, only Dad was charging too much."

"Right. Oh, these are my friends, Emma

and Jamie. We want a word with you."

"Somewhere quiet," Jamie added.

Glen looked puzzled, and a bit suspicious. "What about?" he asked.

"We'll tell you where no one else can hear us," said Jess.

There were three of them and only one of Glen, so he shrugged and went with them to the shade of some trees, out of his dad's earshot.

"OK," he said, "What's this all about?"

"We want to talk about something my mum bought from your pitch," Jess told him. She paused. "The old teddy-bear."

Glen frowned. "Yeah?"

"With a label round its neck." Jess was watching his face carefully. "Ring any bells?"

"Oh, right – I remember. That was your mum, was it? Look, if there's a problem, you'll have to talk to Dad. He—"

"There's a problem all right." Jess interrupted.

"Ah. . ." Glen said.

That was the giveaway. He *did* know something about Bear, and suddenly he looked as if he wanted to run away. But his back was against a tree trunk and the others were blocking his escape, so instead he shifted from foot to foot, trying not to catch anyone's eye.

"You know what I'm on about, don't you?" Jess demanded.

Glen made a mumbling noise that could have meant anything.

"Come on," she continued. "I'll give you a clue, shall I? The clue is: bad luck."

"Oh, hell!" said Glen.

Aha! Jess thought. She signalled to Emma and Jamie, and they all closed in on Glen, who was looking seriously unhappy by now.

"You'd better tell us the truth," Jess said.

"Right," Jamie agreed. " 'Cos, you see, until you do, we're not going anywhere. And neither are you."

Glen's expression was getting more than a bit desperate. "Look," he said, "I can't tell you much, because I don't know anything for sure. But Aunt Lucy once said—"

"Aunt Lucy?" Emma interrupted.

"My great-great-aunt – the one who's just died. All the stuff we're selling was hers. She said—"

"Glen? Glen!" Someone was shouting, and

they looked round to see Glen's dad in the distance. "Come back here!" he called. "You're supposed to be helping, not messing about with your mates!"

Glen looked helplessly at Jess. "I've got to go."

"Not until we've had some answers!" Jamie said fiercely.

"I know, I know! But not here. Look – are you three having a run of bad luck?"

"Are we!" Emma clenched her teeth. "And it all started when—"

"All *right*! I get the message! Listen, what are you doing tomorrow? If we meet up, I'll tell you the story. Deal?"

"*Glen!*" His dad was getting irate.

"Deal," said Jess hastily. "Where, and what time?"

"In the morning; that's best. Eleven o'clock, outside the cinema in the shopping mall."

"We'll be there." Jess paused. "And you'd better be, too!"

"Don't worry," said Glen. "*I* won't chicken out." He started to go, then stopped again. "Oh, one other thing. Don't bring Bear with you. Just *don't*."

And he ran back towards his parents' pitch before any of the others could say a word.

6

In bed that night, Jess lay thinking. Emma and Jamie didn't trust Glen to turn up tomorrow, but she was pretty sure that he would. She'd got the feeling that he *wanted* to talk to them, and he certainly knew something about Bear. "Aunt Lucy said once. . ." he'd begun, but then his dad had interrupted before he could finish. All right, then – they'd find out the rest of it in the morning. For now, she should stop worrying about it and go to sleep.

And try not to think about Glen's last remark: *Don't bring Bear.* As if they would!

But why had he said it?

* * *

She dreamed about the peculiar *thub*bing noise that she'd heard the other night. In the dream she was prowling all round the house and garden trying to find out where the noise came from, but getting nowhere. She was hot, tired and cross; and when she suddenly woke up and realized that it *was* only a dream, she was thoroughly relieved.

But not for long. She'd just shut her eyes to go back to sleep when she heard the noise again.

Thub. Thub.

Only this time, it was real.

"Ohhh!" Jess bit back a rude word. Where *was* that coming from? And what was making it? It was going to get to her if she didn't find out. *When you don't know what something is,* she thought, *you start imagining, don't you? And imagination's always much scarier than reality.*

Thub. Thub. Though it was still a very small noise, it sounded closer than it had been the other night. Jess got out of bed. For a moment, as she took a first step towards the door, a small voice inside her said: *What if. . .?* and she stopped again. *What if what? Don't be such a prat, Jess!*

She crossed the floor and switched the light on. It made her blink but it also made her feel better, and she reached confidently for the door handle. The door opened, spilling brightness on to the landing, and Jess looked out.

There wasn't anything there. She could still hear the noise, though. *Thub. Thub.* It seemed to be coming from the stairs. Weird! What was there on or around the staircase that could possibly make a sound like that?

Jess started to tiptoe along the landing. She wasn't *actually* scared, but she did feel a bit nervous, because she didn't know what she might find. Almost at the top of the stairs now. Another two steps and she'd be able to see down to the hall.

She moved the two last steps, peered over the banisters. . .

And every part of her froze solid.

There was enough moonlight coming through the glass of the front door for her to see all the way down to the hall. Something was on the staircase. Something small, that moved slowly, with a strange, stiff motion.

Thub. Jess's spinning brain couldn't believe it. *Thub.* The sound of something hitting the stair carpet. Something soft. A paw.

Bear was climbing down the stairs.

Jess shoved a clenched fist in her mouth and bit the knuckles so hard that it hurt. It was the only way she could stop herself from screaming the house down. *This isn't happening!* her mind pleaded desperately. *It isn't, it can't be, it's not true!*

But it was true. Bear was *alive*. Hypnotized, Jess stared in blank horror as the small shape heaved itself down another stair. He was making heavy going of it: his arms and legs couldn't bend, so they stuck out awkwardly, and his head wagged from side to side. He still looked like a toy – and that was the most horrible thing of all. Because she knew now that Bear was *not* a toy. He was something else. Something hideous. Something *evil*.

Bear reached the bottom stair. He paused, then rolled over the edge and flopped on to the hall floor, landing on his face. For a moment or two he lay still. Then his arms and legs jerked again, and he hauled himself up until he was standing on his back legs. He started to turn, and with a sudden flash of panic Jess shrank back out of sight. Bear didn't know that anyone was watching him. If he looked up and saw her, she didn't want to imagine what he would – or could – do.

Thub. Thub. He must be walking along the hall. *Don't look, Jess! Don't look, don't make a sound, don't do anything at all!* Then there was a faint creak, as if the sitting-room door had been eased open. *Thub. Thub.* Jess held her breath. The sound was fading away, and at last there was silence.

She counted to fifty before she dared peer cautiously over the banisters again. The hall below was empty now. Bear had gone. But the sitting-room door was ajar.

A frightened little whimper crept out of Jess's mouth. Her heart was lurching and bumping under her ribs; she was too scared to move and yet too scared to stay where she was. She looked over her shoulder and saw the light coming from her bedroom. Friendly light – safe light! If she could just make her legs work. . .

She made it back to the room in a sudden tiptoeing rush, and flung herself down on her bed, scrabbling the duvet over her and hiding beneath it. She couldn't think straight. No one could, if they'd just seen what she had! But one awful question was thundering in her mind. Bear had been going *down* the stairs. Which meant that he must have come *up*stairs to start with.

Why? What did he want?

And what had he been *doing*?

She grabbed her personal stereo, jammed the earphones in and found a radio station that was playing really loud music. If anything else happened tonight, she didn't want to hear it. She didn't want to *know* about it. Tomorrow, she'd ask Mum if she could have a bolt on her bedroom door, and if Mum said no, she'd buy one herself.

Jess shut her eyes, listening to the blare of the music, and tried to think about something – anything – that was dull and boring and ordinary.

As they headed for the cinema the next morning, Jess desperately wanted to tell Emma and Jamie about last night, but she didn't know where to start. "I woke up and heard this noise, and I saw Bear walking around the house." Oh, great. They'd say she was dreaming. This morning she'd almost believed that herself, for a while. But only for a while.

Glen was waiting outside the cinema, as he'd promised. He looked fidgety and jumpy, and as they came up to him, his first question was: "You didn't bring Bear, did you?"

Jess's heart skipped. "Of course we didn't!" she snapped. "We said we wouldn't. Anyway, who'd want to?"

"Yeah. Yeah, right. Look, I've been thinking about this. And I want you to come somewhere with me."

"Oh?" Emma looked interested but wary. "Where?"

"Aunt Lucy's house," said Glen.

Three faces goggled at him and Jamie opened his mouth, but before he could speak, Glen hurried on.

"Mum and Dad usually go there on Sundays to sort through things, but they're getting fed up with it so this week they've gone out for the day instead. I've got the key. And I think it'd be the best place to talk."

They thought about it for a few moments.

Then Emma said cautiously, "OK. If it helps, we'll come. How far is it?"

"We can walk it from here." Glen jerked his head in the direction of the high street. "Come on."

They didn't talk much on the way to the house. Emma tried, once, to start Glen on the subject of Aunt Lucy, but he said he'd rather wait until they got there before anyone said anything. So they concentrated on the walk, and at last, when they'd reached a quiet area with no shops, Glen stopped.

"This is her road," he said. "The house is number nine, just up there."

They looked where he pointed. This was the smart end of town. The houses were all detached and Victorian, and stood in their own gardens. Trees lined the street, and there was no one around. Aunt Lucy must have been pretty well off, Jess thought.

All the same, number nine was a lot less smart than the others in the street. In fact, as Glen opened the front gate, Jess decided that there was something dead creepy about it. The garden hedge and trees had grown so high that you couldn't see the neighbours, and everything looked grubby and neglected. A huge creeper grew over the front, nearly covering the windows, and when Glen opened the door it creaked and groaned like the door of a spooky castle in a horror movie.

"The electricity's been turned off," he said as they groped their way into the gloomy interior. "Sorry. We'll just have to manage without any lights."

The morning was sunny, so that shouldn't have been a problem. But the overgrown creeper and the crowding trees cut out so much daylight that everything was shrouded in a dismal, green-tinged gloom, and shadows loomed in every corner.

Uneasily, they all looked around. They were in a big hall, with dark walls and a high ceiling. There wasn't any furniture, and doors stood open, showing glimpses of bare, bleak rooms. There was a damp, mildewy smell, and the atmosphere was very depressing. Emma shuddered and muttered under her breath, and Jess felt as if something slimy had started to crawl over her skin. She didn't want to be here. She wished they hadn't come.

Glen turned and looked at them. There was an odd, grim expression on his face. Then he spread his hands wide and said, "Well, this is it. Aunt Lucy's house. The place where she had all her bad luck. . ."

7

They stood in the big sitting-room. There was no furniture in here, either. The walls were painted a murky pea-green and a grimy bay window looked out over the garden. Jess was feeling worse and worse every minute. She thought this was just about the most depressing place she'd ever seen, and it was all she could do not to turn and run outside again.

Jamie looked at Glen, who was staring out of the window. "All right," he said. "So what exactly do you mean about your Aunt Lucy?"

Glen took a deep breath. "It might not be true, of course. I mean, it's not the sort of thing anyone with any sense'd believe. But. . ."

"Try us," Emma put in sharply.

Glen sighed. "OK. Here goes, then."

Aunt Lucy, he said, had been his dad's great-aunt, and had lived in this house all her life. "It was her parents' place, and because she never got married, they left it to her when they died. She lived here on her own for years. Then, when *she* died, Dad was her nearest relation, so he inherited it all."

He started to pace round the room. "If you think it looks weird now, you should have seen it when Aunt Lucy was alive. It was full of old stuff that'd been in the family since the Ark. Dad's got rid of most of the things from down here, but upstairs it's like a cross between a junk shop and a museum. I'll show you in a bit."

Jess didn't want to be shown, but she said nothing. Glen continued.

"Aunt Lucy was pretty OK, really, though in the end she went a bit – well, not exactly funny, but eccentric, I suppose. She used to love telling stories about the past, but some of the ones she told were pretty weird. You know, didn't make much sense. Mum and Dad hated hearing them, but I sort of enjoyed it. That's why Aunt Lucy liked me."

"And she told you something about Bear?" Emma asked.

"Not exactly," said Glen. "All she said was that there was something in the house that brought bad luck. She wouldn't say what it was. But I tell you, Aunt Lucy was *unlucky*!"

The three friends exchanged glances. "Unlucky," Jamie repeated. "What – um – sort of unlucky?"

Glen shoved his hands into his pockets. "Just about every way you could think of. She kept having accidents – you know, tripping over, losing her purse, breaking ornaments. They were the small bits of bad luck. Then there were the big ones."

There was a sharp silence. An emergency vehicle went by in the distance, its siren screaming, and Jess shivered. Then Glen said, "She got engaged in the 1930s. Then the Second World War started, and her fiancé joined the RAF and got killed."

"That happened to loads of people," Jamie pointed out.

"I know. But then she met someone else.

66

That was in the war, too. He was a train driver, and one day he swapped shifts because another driver had flu. The train he was driving got a direct hit from a bomb. Right in the cab." Glen shrugged. "He shouldn't have been on that train at all. Then the third guy she met—"

"You mean, it happened to her *three* times?" Emma said in horrified astonishment.

Glen nodded. "The third one got killed in a car crash. Weird thing was, he wasn't supposed to be in the car, just like the train driver. It was a business trip, and the guy who should have been going couldn't make it at the last minute. So after that, Aunt Lucy sort of gave up. She said to me once – she said she didn't want to kill anyone else."

The others were very quiet for a while. And the atmosphere in the house seemed to be getting gloomier. At last, Emma asked quietly, "What else happened to her?"

As if that wasn't enough, Jess thought. Glen glanced at her, as if he guessed what she was thinking, and said, "Loads of things. Like a really serious illness – she got better, but she could never walk properly afterwards. And she lost a whole lot of money; lent it to someone, and they cheated her, and she never got it back. Stuff like that, you know."

"How old was she when she died?" Emma wanted to know.

"Nearly ninety."

"Nearly . . . *whoo!*" Emma went pale, and Jess and Jamie knew what was going through her mind. To be jinxed all those years, and never be free of it − it was absolutely *horrifying*.

Glen stopped pacing at last, and stood by the door. "Like I said, Aunt Lucy believed her bad luck was caused by something in the house, but she'd never tell me what it was."

"You didn't work out that it was Bear, then?" Emma sounded surprised. "I'd have thought that label round his neck was a dead giveaway!"

"I'd never seen Bear," Glen said. "I don't think Mum or Dad had, either. But when I *did* see him, and read what was on that label. . ." He shrugged uncomfortably. "It didn't take Einstein to put two and two together."

"What did your mum and dad think about it?" Emma asked.

"They didn't take any notice. Just thought it was some old joke. They sort of liked Bear, though. They thought about keeping him, but then Mum said it was a shame to leave him stuck on a shelf when some little kid would love to have him to play with."

Jess gave a hollow laugh, and Jamie said, "Oh, *great!*"

"I know," Glen agreed. "Bear gave me the creeps right from the start. I wouldn't even touch him."

It was all starting to fit, Jess thought. Glen's parents had liked Bear, so although they'd handled him, he hadn't put his hex on them. Glen didn't like him, but he'd managed to avoid touching him, and had escaped the jinx. It made a hideous kind of sense.

Glen was talking again. "When Dad sold Bear to Jess's mum, I was just glad to get rid of him. But then you came along yesterday, asking questions." He grimaced. "I wanted to pretend I didn't know anything about it. But that wouldn't have been fair, would it?"

"Not if your Aunt Lucy had bad luck all her life, it wouldn't!" Emma agreed fiercely. "We thought it'd wear off after a while! Now, though. . ." She looked into a grisly future, stretching out ahead of them all. "What are we going to do?"

"Why didn't Aunt Lucy just throw him away?" Jamie wanted to know. "That would've been the best way out of it."

"I think she was too scared of him." Glen looked Jamie in the eye. "Aren't you?"

Jamie didn't answer, but his face went a bit red.

"There you are then," said Glen. "You daren't get rid of him because of what might happen. Aunt Lucy was the same. At least. . ." He stopped.

"At least what?" said Emma.

Glen swallowed. "I think she *did* try. Right at the end, just before she was taken in to hospital. I saw her then, you see – I came here with Mum to help the ambulance people. Aunt Lucy said something to me. She was pretty far gone by then, and her mind was wandering, but she said, 'I tried to find it, Glen. I wanted to get rid of it for good and all, to stop it harming anyone else. But I can't find it. I've looked everywhere, but it's gone.' She must have meant Bear, mustn't she?"

"Sounds like it," said Jamie. "Did she say anything else?"

He shook his head. "No. But. . ." Then his voice tailed off again. Suddenly he looked very twitchy, and Jess felt an awful surge of intuition.

"What were you going to say?" she asked sharply.

It was the first time she'd spoken since they reached the house, and Emma and Jamie looked at her in surprise. Jess ignored them. She was only interested in Glen, and Glen knew it.

He said uncomfortably, "It doesn't matter. It isn't anything important."

Oh, isn't it? thought Jess. Her heart was thumping with a queasy, nervy sensation. She knew Glen was holding something back, and she wanted to find out what it was.

"Tell me!" she demanded.

Glen was really squirming now. "Look," he said, "this doesn't make any sense."

"Just *tell* me!" said Jess.

He gave in. "All right. And if you think I'm crazy, then tough." His shoulders heaved. "She'd tried to find Bear, to get rid of him, but she couldn't. She was worried." He looked at them in turn, edgily. "When Mum was getting her ready for the ambulance, she wanted some things from her dressing table. I got them for her. So I *saw* what was on there. Then Mum and I went to the hospital with her, and afterwards we came back here." There was a long pause. "When we went up to her room, Bear was sitting on the dressing table."

Emma frowned. "He must have been there before. You just didn't notice."

"Don't be stupid! How could I have missed something that size? Look, if you don't believe me, then—"

"I believe you," Jess interrupted.

Emma and Jamie stared at her. "Oh, come on!" Jamie snorted. "That's completely wacko! What d'you think he did – hide in the wardrobe till everyone had gone away? He's only a toy; he can't get up and move around by himself!"

Jess took a very deep breath and said: "Oh, yes he can."

8

Emma and Jamie didn't believe it, of course. Just as Jess had expected, they told her it must have been a nightmare. Jamie even laughed, though the laugh was more like a nervous giggle. But as Jess argued, Glen suddenly said, "*I* believe her."

The others stopped squabbling and stared at him. "What?" said Emma incredulously.

"I said, I believe Jess." Glen squared up to Emma and Jamie. "Look what happened to me. How did Bear get on to Aunt Lucy's dressing table when there was no one around to put him there? He walked, that's how! It's the only explanation."

"Oh, rubbish!" said Emma scornfully. "Of course it isn't!"

"Well, you tell me another one, then."

Emma opened her mouth, then realized that she couldn't explain it. It didn't make sense. But what other possible explanation was there?

"Look," Glen said, "I don't know how bad Bear can make things for people he doesn't like, but I reckon it'd be a big mistake to rule anything out." He lowered his voice, as if some unseen listener might be lurking in the shadows. "That's why I wanted you to come here. Bear's got to go, before things get any worse. The problem is how to do it safely. I've got an idea, but it'd take ages on my own. Four of us'd stand a much better chance."

"What is it?" Jess asked eagerly.

"Aunt Lucy told me once that Bear was already pretty old when she got him," said Glen. "Someone gave him to her when she was a kid."

Emma pulled a face. "Brilliant! With friends like that, who needs enemies?"

"Yeah, well, maybe they didn't know about the jinx," Glen went on. "Or maybe they did.

So, like I said earlier, Aunt Lucy lived in this house all her life, and so did her parents. And up in the attic there's boxes and boxes of old papers and letters and stuff, that go right back to the year dot."

Jess began to see what he was getting at. "You mean, there might be some clues in them?"

Glen nodded. "Dad hasn't even started looking through them yet. So if *we* did. . ."

"We might find something that tells us how to get rid of Bear!"

"Exactly," said Glen, "like, fr'instance, another clue from whoever put the label round his neck!"

Jess and her friends looked at each other. It was a chance. Of course there might not be anything, and they'd only waste hours of time and energy. But it was worth a try.

"OK," said Jamie at last. "I'm up for it. When do we start?"

"Sooner the better," Emma urged. "Before we have any more bad luck!"

As she said that, something clicked in Jess's mind. A thought had been nagging away at her, but she hadn't been able to grasp it.

Now, suddenly, she realized what it was.

"Hang on a minute," she said. "Has anyone noticed anything weird?"

"Like what?" Jamie asked. "Everything in this house is weird, if you ask me!"

"I don't mean that. It was what Emma said just now, about bad luck. It's just that we don't seem to have had any today."

There was a moment's silence. Then: "You're right," Emma said. "Nothing's happened. No accidents, no near-misses." Her eyes widened. "Do you think the jinx has gone?"

"No, I don't." Jess glanced at Glen and saw that he agreed. "It's more as if it's . . . paused for a bit. But I can't work out why."

"That's spooky," Emma whispered.

"I know. And I don't think we ought to hang around. I think we ought to get going on Glen's idea right now." She shuddered. "Before the jinx starts up again."

Any notion that Aunt Lucy's attic could be searched in a few hours flew straight out of the window when they saw the place.

The room ran the whole length and width of

the house, and it was packed to the rafters. Furniture, books, pictures, clothes, ornaments – you name it, it was there. Quite a lot of objects were damaged, and some had inexplicable dark streaks and smears, like soot, on them. But the undamaged stuff – well, it was amazing. There was even an old wooden rocking-horse with a moth-eaten mane and tail and a nasty look in its eyes. At any other time, Jess and her friends would have loved to be let loose among it all. Now, though, the prospect of hunting through it was nightmarish.

There were eight boxes and chests of papers, all covered in dust and cobwebs. Glen reckoned they went back at least a hundred years. Aunt Lucy must have been the sort of person who never threw anything away.

They got started – and they got nowhere. The first box was stuffed with old bills and solicitors' letters, some of them even written by hand. They had to go through it all, just in case, and by the time they finished everyone was hot and dusty and tempers were getting short.

Jamie looked at his watch, and was astonished. "It's a quarter to four! We've taken hours, and we've only done one box!"

"I can't start another one," Emma wailed. "Not now!"

The others agreed, and Glen said his parents would be home soon anyway, and he ought to get back.

"What about tomorrow?" Jess asked. "Shall we have another go then?"

Glen nodded. "I think we should. Meet me here as early as you can, and we can have the whole day. Oh, and you'd better bring sarnies or something; there's no takeaways for miles."

Jamie groaned. "I'm starving now!"

"Well, come on, let's go." Now that they'd stopped searching, Jess just wanted to get away from this creepy house with all its memories. She stood up, brushed dust from herself and stared around the attic. The sun had gone from the window and it looked gloomy and a little bit threatening.

They climbed down the steep, narrow attic stairway. It was a relief to be outside in the bright daylight. Glen locked the house up, then said, "See you tomorrow, then. And . . . be careful, huh?"

Emma squeaked, "Don't!" with a shiver, but

Jess nodded. "Yeah, we will." She thought about the mysterious lack of accidents so far today, and added, "*Very* careful."

There weren't any accidents for the rest of that day. None at all. By mid-evening Jess was so twitchy about it that she rang Emma and Jamie to see if anything had happened to them. Nothing had. It was uncanny.

She went to bed feeling as if her nerves were plugged into the electric circuit. No way would she be able to sleep – not after what had gone on last night. Would Bear walk again? Part of Jess didn't want to know the answer, but another part desperately did. Because she was terrified that, if he did walk, he would come upstairs and get into her room. How could any-one in their right mind get to sleep with that threat hanging over them?

So she gathered up books, magazines, puzzles – anything that would keep her busy – and piled them on the bed with her. No tapes or CDs, though. If Bear crept up the stairs, she wanted to hear him coming.

Time crawled by. Eventually the muffled sound of the downstairs TV stopped, and a few minutes later Mum and Dad went to bed. Jess turned her light off for a minute in case Mum looked in, and breathed a sigh of relief when footsteps tiptoed past without stopping. She heard the loo flush, and water running in the bathroom basin. Then the house was silent.

But not for long.

Cre-e-e-ak.

It sounded like the sitting-room door easing open. Jess's heart walloped against her ribs. Had she imagined it? She tensed, listening hard. Then:

Thub.

Jess held her breath. She could feel herself starting to shake, and tried to stop. But she couldn't.

Thub. It was such a small noise, and yet it was the most menacing sound that Jess had ever heard in her life.

Thub. Thub.

"Oh, God!" The whisper came out so thinly that Jess could hardly hear it herself. She wished that someone else was here – Emma, Jamie, Glen – someone who'd *believe* this. But there was only Mum and Dad, and she couldn't call out to them. She just *couldn't*. She was on her own.

She slid out of bed and padded towards the door as if she was walking on hot embers. Bear mustn't know she was awake, or – or she didn't know what, but he *mustn't* find out that she knew about his night prowling. Luckily, her bedroom door didn't creak the way the downstairs one did. She turned the light off again (it took some nerve to do that), then opened the door a crack and peered out on to the dark landing.

Thub. She could hear it more clearly now. He was definitely on the stairs, heading this way. And there was a glimmer of light showing at the top of the staircase. It flickered and wavered, but it was too yellow to be moonlight. What on earth was it?

Then suddenly, Jess guessed what the flickering light was. A flame. A real one. It was crazy, and she could be wrong, but an awful intuition told her she wasn't.

Horror hit her, and she knew she had to find out for sure. She dropped to her knees and started to crawl slowly, carefully, along the landing. The stairs looked a billion miles away, but the steady *thub . . . thub . . .* seemed terrifyingly loud at floor level. Yet she had to go on. She had to *know*.

She was only a metre from the top of the staircase now. How far up was Bear? Impossible to tell: he could be less than half-way, or nearly at the top. *Go on, Jess! You've got to!*

She crawled another step, then another, and another. Almost there. If she raised her head very carefully, and looked. . .

She did.

And froze.

Bear was there. He was four stairs from the top of the flight, and as Jess looked, he heaved himself clumsily up another step. He was very clumsy tonight because in one front paw, he was carrying a lit candle.

Jess couldn't stop herself. She gave a gasp that hissed sharply in the silence.

And Bear heard her.

In one rigid, terrified moment, Jess saw Bear lift his head and glare up to the landing. His beady eyes fixed on her face, and they seemed to glow with a ghastly light of their own. Their gazes locked, and Jess thought she saw Bear's mouth twist into a hideous leer. But that was impossible! Bear didn't have a mouth: his face was just a piece of *stitching*; it wasn't *real*.

Dizzy with panic, but unable to move a muscle, Jess opened her own mouth, knowing she was going to scream. Bear's paw moved so fast that it was a blur—

And he stubbed out the candle he was holding, plunging the landing into darkness.

"*No-o-o-o!*" The spell that hypnotized Jess shattered, and she leaped to her feet and went pelting back to her room. Punching the light on, she flung herself on to the bed.

"Jess, is that you? Are you all right?"

Mum came hurrying in through the doorway. "Jess! Whatever's the matter?"

Jess wanted to say: *He's there, he's alive and he's on the stairs! Go and LOOK!* But right now she was too upset to say anything at all.

"Was it a bad dream?" Mum asked sympathetically. "Poor old you! Never mind; you're awake now." She sat on the edge of the bed until Jess had calmed down a bit, then said soothing things and went away. When she'd gone, Jess lay very still, listening, but there were no more noises from the stairs. *No*, she thought, trying to stop the shaking that had hold of her, *there wouldn't be, would there*?

Bear would be back downstairs, back on his shelf, looking innocent and normal. He wouldn't try to get upstairs again tonight. He wouldn't try to do anything else.

But *he* knew that *she* knew the truth about him. And that was the most frightening thing of all. Because it meant that when he *did* strike back – and he would – he'd strike hard.

Harder than he'd ever done before. . .

9

Jess didn't get a wink of sleep for the rest of that night. She lay in bed with the light on and her duvet wrapped round her like a cocoon, staring at the wall and trying not to think.

But of course she did think. It was impossible not to. And before long a terrifying question occurred to her.

Why had Bear been carrying a candle? She didn't believe for a moment that he needed it to see by, and it had obviously made climbing a lot harder for him. So why had he wanted it? There was only one obvious answer.

He'd been planning to set something on fire.

Jess remembered the clutter in the attic at Aunt Lucy's house. Some of the things up there had had black smears and streaks on them. Scorch marks? Had there ever been a fire at the house?

Jess sat bolt upright in bed as the full horror of that thought hit her. Was *that* what Bear had been going to do? Had he been about to set the house ablaze, with her and Mum and Dad asleep (or so Bear thought) inside?

"*He wouldn't. . .*" she whispered aloud. *Oh, wouldn't he?* a small inner voice replied silently. No accidents for the past couple of days. As if Bear was biding his time. Waiting to do something worse.

And now, Bear knew that she had seen him.

Jess's heart started to pound so hard that she thought she was going to throw up. She didn't, but the pounding continued dizzily. She had to do something. And there was only one thing that made sense, terrifying though the thought of it was.

She had to do what Aunt Lucy had failed to do. She had to get rid of Bear.

Instantly, all the things that she and Emma and Jamie had said came piling back into her mind. *It's too dangerous – we can't risk it – what if he takes revenge somehow?* But if something wasn't done, and fast, the danger might be much greater. Jess believed she had no choice. Bear had to *go*.

How to do it, though? Throwing him away was no good; he could easily escape from a dustbin or whatever, and come back. No, he had to be *destroyed*. And she had to plan it so that Bear wouldn't realize what was going on until it was too late.

She lay awake wrestling with the problem, but by dawn she hadn't come up with an answer. As light started to creep into her room, she got up and went to the window. The garden might give her an idea.

She looked outside. The shed – no use. The pond – but you couldn't drown something that wasn't alive, could you? It might work, but the risk was too great. Her gaze strayed over the fence. And there was the answer staring her in the face.

There was a big pile of rubbish in the next-door garden. That could only mean one thing – Bonfire Bill was going to make a nuisance of himself again.

It was the perfect solution! That bonfire would be set alight later today. And if Bear was right in the middle of it, even he wouldn't be able to escape!

Jess grabbed her clothes, flung them on and crept downstairs. She had to steady her nerves before she went into the sitting-room, but with a great effort she managed it, and quickly switched the light on.

Bear was back on his shelf. The candle was back in its holder, too, though when Jess looked at it she saw that the wick was blackened, showing that it had been lit. It was the final proof that she hadn't dreamed it. And it bolstered her courage.

She looked at Bear and made herself smile. "Dear Bear," she said. "*Nice* Bear." She didn't really think he'd be fooled, but it was worth a try. "Aren't you a clever Bear?" she said, and started to reach out. . .

Oops, Jess! Don't touch him! Gloves, gloves – she ran to the kitchen and found some rubber household ones. She found a couple of other things, too. A length of string, and a roll of bandage from the first-aid drawer.

Putting the gloves on, she went back to the

sitting-room and took Bear down from the shelf. His eyes didn't seem so unnerving this morning; in fact they looked like an ordinary toy's eyes. *You don't fool me*, Jess thought grimly. She took the string and wound it round and round him, tying his legs together and his arms to his sides. Right. That put paid to any walking. Then she wrapped the bandage over his eyes, so that he couldn't see anything either. There was one creepy moment when she thought that Bear gave a wriggle, as if he was objecting, but she managed to convince herself she'd imagined it. OK. All ready. Now all she had to do was take him next door.

The garden gate squeaked, so Jess climbed over the fence and crept towards the bonfire. She kept a wary eye out for any lights or twitching curtains in Bonfire Bill's house, but it was too early for anyone to be awake. The bonfire was a big one, and she rummaged into the centre of it, making a hole big enough to put Bear in.

Bear didn't do anything. He just lay there, tied up and blindfolded, as Jess carefully rearranged the pile so that he was completely hidden. She had a panicky moment as she

89

finished, wondering if this was the biggest mistake she'd ever made in her life. But the feeling passed after a minute, and she scrambled back over the fence and up to her room again.

She actually managed to fall asleep, but not for long. Suddenly Mum – who had just got up – came storming in.

"All right, where is he?" she demanded.

Jess blinked blearily and sat up. For a moment she didn't know what Mum was on about. Then she remembered.

"Where's who?" she said, trying desperately to sound baffled.

"Bear, of course!" Mum was hopping mad. "And don't tell me it wasn't you, because it couldn't have been anybody else!"

"Bear?" echoed Jess, playing innocent. "What's happened?"

"You know perfectly well!" Mum snarled. "What have you done with him?"

"I haven't done anything with him, Mum. Honest!"

"Oh, yes you have! You took him off his shelf and put him somewhere!" Mum's eyebrows knitted together threateningly. "And I want him back!"

Jess stuck to her story, insisting that she had nothing to do with Bear's disappearance. She didn't usually tell lies, and Mum wanted to believe her. But Mum couldn't think of any other explanation. She towed Jess all round the house as she turned it upside down looking for Bear. But of course she didn't find him, and in the end she said in a hurt voice, "I'm very upset, Jess! It isn't like you to do something behind my back and then tell fibs about it!"

"But Mum—"

"Don't argue; I don't want to hear any more! You may not like Bear, but I do, and he belongs to me. I don't know where you've hidden him, but I want him back. Do you understand?"

Jess said nothing.

"Right." Mum wagged a finger at the alcove. "I expect to see him back on that shelf by this evening! And then you'll tell me why you did it. And I want the truth!"

She stomped out of the sitting-room, leaving Jess alone. Jess looked out of the window. She could just see the garden next door, and she thought she glimpsed Bonfire Bill out there already. She felt a pang of guilt – not about

Bear, only about the fact that she'd lied to Mum.

"*Sorry, Mum,*" she whispered. "*But maybe I'll be able to tell you about it one day.*"

Or maybe she never, ever would. . .

Jess pretended she didn't want any breakfast, and managed to avoid her parents until Dad had left for work. As soon as the coast was clear in the kitchen, she went to make herself some toast. She was so preoccupied with watching for the first signs of Bonfire Bill lighting up that she didn't concentrate, and when she heard the toast pop up, she reached for it without looking.

Her hand came down slap on the hot top of the toaster.

Jess yelped and jumped backwards as a burning pain shot through her scorched fingers. She was sucking them and rummaging in the drawer for burn ointment when Mum came in.

"Whatever have you done?" Then Mum saw. "Oh, no! Quick, hold your hand under the cold tap!" Suddenly she wasn't cross any more, only concerned. Tears filled Jess's eyes. Telling herself that it was only the pain making her cry, she stood still while Mum salved her fingers. Luckily the burns weren't bad, and by the time Mum had finished they only stung a bit.

But all the while Jess was thinking: *My first accident since the day before yesterday. It's only a coincidence. It can't be anything to do with Bear. . .*

She looked out of the window again. Bonfire Bill still hadn't got his fire going. *Come on, come on!* Jess urged him silently. She should be on her way to Aunt Lucy's house by now, to meet Emma and Jamie and Glen. But she needed to see that fire start burning. Just to be absolutely sure.

As if her prayers had been answered, Bonfire Bill appeared at that moment, with a can of paraffin in his hand. Whistling cheerfully, he walked to the bonfire and carefully sprinkled some paraffin on the pile. Then he lit a piece of rag and, using long tongs, thrust it into the heap.

Relief flooded Jess as yellow flames began to lick upwards. From upstairs she heard Mum say furiously, "Oh, not again!" and the slam of windows being shut. Jess only smiled. This morning, Bonfire Bill could smoke the whole street out for all she cared!

Feeling more light-hearted than she'd done for ages, she left the house. She went out by the back way, just so that she could call a sunny "Hello!" to Bonfire Bill. He waved back, and Jess went running, almost skipping, towards town and Aunt Lucy's house.

She vanished, and Bonfire Bill poked and prodded at his fire. It was going very well now, with plenty of flame and lots of smoke. Right in the heart of it were a length of string and a piece of bandage. If anyone had seen the string before it shrivelled up and burned, they might have noticed that it looked chewed.

Bonfire Bill whistled happily. He didn't hear a soft rustling in the shrubs at one side of his garden. And he didn't hear a strange little noise. A sort of *thub . . . thub. . .*

As if a small *something* was creeping along by the fence. . .

10

Glen opened the door of Aunt Lucy's house when he saw Jess coming.

"Hi," he said. "We wondered where you'd got to."

"Sorry!" Jess had been running, and was out of breath. She rushed into the bare hall, which didn't seem half so gloomy as it had done yesterday. "Have I got something to tell you!"

Emma and Jamie appeared from the sitting-room, and they all crowded round. "What's happened?" Jamie asked, and Emma added worriedly, "Have there been more accidents?"

"No! Well. . ." Jess waved her burnt fingers. "Just this, but it doesn't matter; I'll tell you about it later." She paused to take a deep breath. "Bear's gone. For *good!*"

Amid all the questions that came piling in, she managed to explain the whole story. Emma had a bad attack of the shivers when Jess described how Bear had seen her as he crept up the stairs, and when finally she told them about the bonfire, Glen and Jamie both whistled softly.

"God!" said Jamie admiringly. "That took some guts, Jess! What if he'd—"

"Shut up!" Jess interrupted hastily. "I don't even want to think about that!"

Glen, his face serious, said, "And the bonfire was burning – really burning – when you left?"

"Yeah." Jess nodded. "Bear's gone. We've got rid of him."

"But Jess, wasn't it dangerous?" Emma said, in a scared voice. "After what we said about revenge—"

"I don't care!" Jess snapped. "He knew I'd seen him – it would've been much more dangerous *not* to do it!"

"So: no more Bear, no more accidents!"

Jamie had begun to grin. "I reckon we ought to celebrate!"

Emma nodded dubiously. But Glen was frowning, and he pointed at Jess's hand. "You haven't told us about that yet."

"Oh – it wasn't anything. I just scorched myself a bit on the toaster, 'cos I didn't look what I was doing."

"When?" asked Glen.

"This morning – oh, I get it!" Jess grinned. "It's OK. It was *before* Bonfire Bill lit his fire." Then her face sobered. "I suppose it could have been Bear. His last attack, sort of thing. Ugh!" She shuddered. "Let's not talk about it any more. We've got rid of him. That's what matters."

"Well!" said Jamie, heaving a big sigh. "So what are we going to do now?" He stared round the room. "Can we look around the house a bit more, Glen? Now I'm not scared of it, I want to see what else is here."

"Me, too!" Emma agreed. "There was some amazing stuff in the attic."

"OK, if you want." Glen looked at Jess, who shrugged and said, "Suits me." As Jamie said, there was nothing to be scared of any more. It might even be fun.

The four of them clattered up the bare wooden stairs to the attic. This time they ignored the boxes of papers, and started instead to rummage through the other piles. At first Jess was a bit uneasy, but after a while the feeling wore off. After all, it was hardly likely that Aunt Lucy had had any other jinxed toys. Bear was a one-off. *Go on, Jess*, she told herself. *Stop being twitchy, and enjoy it!*

They found the big wooden chest a few minutes later. It had been shoved right against one wall, behind some stacked pictures. The chest had had designs painted on it once, and though the paint was flaked and faded they could just make out what some of the designs were. A rabbit. A bat and ball. An old-fashioned spinning top. . .

"Wow!" said Glen. "It must be the old family toy-box! Dad said there were toys here going back to the year dot."

"Let's have a look," Emma urged.

Between them they heaved the chest out into the middle of the floor. The catch had rusted, but Glen found a hammer, and a few bashes broke the old metal.

It *was* a toy-box, and a lot of toys were still in it.

"Hey, look at this!" Jamie pulled out what looked like a big wooden houseboat. "Cool!"

"It's a Noah's Ark," said Emma. "Here are the animals – look." She plonked a tiger, a zebra and something that looked vaguely like a hippopotamus beside the boat.

Jess lifted up a doll. It had a china head and real hair, and it was dressed in Edwardian clothes. Everything in here was very old, she realized – maybe even older than Aunt Lucy.

"Oh, look at this!" Emma cried delightedly. She was holding a little box, covered with velvet on which pictures had been painted. When she lifted the lid, the tiny figure of a ballerina rose up from inside, and a faint tune tinkled tremulously for a few seconds before slowing down and stopping.

"I remember that!" Glen said. "Aunt Lucy's musical box – she used to keep it on her mantelpiece." He fished inside. "There should be a key somewhere, to wind it up . . . yeah, here it is."

He slotted the key into a small hole and turned it a few times. The tune began to play again, and the tiny ballerina turned round and round.

"One of her aunts gave it to her, she said," Glen went on. Then he frowned. "It used to belong to someone else, but I can't remember who."

No one took much notice of him. Emma was enchanted with the musical box, while Jess and Jamie were delving deeper into the toy-chest. More Ark animals, four wooden soldiers, a skipping rope, some lacy clothes that could have been for a doll or a real baby. . . Then Jess glimpsed a bundle of papers right at the bottom. Her hand moved towards it – then she jumped as from somewhere downstairs came a loud metallic rattle.

Emma and Jamie had jumped too, and they all stared nervously at each other. "*What was that?*" Emma hissed.

"Uh?" Glen looked up. "Postman." He saw their faces and grinned. "Stuff still gets delivered for Aunt Lucy, and the letter-box flap makes a noise like the Voice of Doom."

"Oh!" Jess felt stupid.

"It scared me the first few times I heard it!" Glen's grin grew wider and he stood up. "I'll go and see, in case it's anything for Dad to sort out."

"I'll come too," said Jess. "I want to go to the loo. Does the water still work?"

"Yeah, should do. Come on then, and I'll show you where it is."

The bathroom was on the next floor down, and the water did work. When she came out, Jess met Glen coming back. He looked puzzled.

"There isn't any post," he told her.

"Oh. So what was the noise?"

"It *was* the letter-box. Couldn't have been anything else. But nothing's been put through. There's just some leaves and twigs and bits on the mat." Glen shrugged. "Maybe it was little kids being stupid – my sister does that sort of thing. Funny we didn't hear them coming up the path, though."

They went back upstairs. In the attic, Emma and Jamie had delved deeper into the box, and the pile of old toys was spreading out around them.

"You'd never think it could hold so much, would you?" said Emma.

Jamie grinned. "The box is a Tardis. If we

get inside and shut the lid, we'll end up on some other planet, surrounded by aliens!"

Jess and Glen joined in again and they carried on rummaging. The bundle of papers Jess had seen earlier seemed to have disappeared, but she was too fascinated by all the other things to even remember it.

They'd almost got to the very bottom of the chest when she thought she heard another sound from downstairs. Jess sat back on her heels, frowning, and Emma gave her a curious look.

"What's up, Jess?"

"Did you just hear something?" Jess asked.

"Like what?"

"Probably kids at the letter-box again," said Glen.

Jess shook her head. "It was a different noise. A sort of . . . thumping."

They all listened for a few moments. Then Jamie said, "Nah. You must've imagined it, Jess."

"Or maybe it was the wind blowing something," Glen suggested. "Loads of windows are cracked, and there's draughts all over the place."

The others agreed that must have been it,

and soon they were all absorbed in their exploration again.

Then the third disturbance happened.

This time it wasn't a noise, but a smell. Jamie noticed it first. He raised his head and started sniffing, like a dog passing a butcher's shop. Emma glanced at him and said, "If you've got a cold, don't you dare give it to me!"

"I haven't." Jamie was still sniffing. "I was just wondering where that's coming from."

"Where what's coming from?" Jess sniffed, too. "Oh, right. That smell. Yuk!" She grinned wryly. "It makes me think of. . ."

She stopped. The others looked at her. Emma prompted, "What?"

Jess swallowed. She'd been going to say that the smell made her think of Bonfire Bill. But just as the words came, she'd realized why. She'd realized what the smell was.

Suddenly agitated, she looked quickly round the attic – and saw what was rising up through the floorboards. Grey and vague and drifting, it looked like mist. But it wasn't.

"Oh, God!" Jess leaped to her feet, her voice rising to a yelp. "Look, *look*! It's smoke! *There's a fire downstairs!*"

11

As they rushed down the attic stairs, a dark column of smoke billowed up from the hall, and the stench of burning made their nostrils curl.

"Quick!" Glen yelled. "We need something to smother it!" He tore into one of the bedrooms and wrenched the curtains down from the windows. Emma ran to another room and grabbed a bedspread, then all four of them scrambled down to the ground floor.

The fire had started near the door of the big, empty room with the bay windows. Luckily, there was much more smoke than flame –

whatever had caught alight must have been damp, and wouldn't burn properly. Glen flung the curtains over it, and Emma dumped the bedspread on top. Then, while Jamie trampled on the heap, the other three fetched pans and buckets from the kitchen and poured water over everything.

They kept trampling and pouring until they were sure that the very last smouldering fragment was out. Then, gingerly, Glen pulled the soaked coverings away and everyone peered at the soggy mess underneath.

"It looks like paper," Jamie said.

"Yeah," Glen agreed. He looked bemused. "But how did it get there?"

"Maybe your mum and dad put it there," Emma suggested. "You know – for wrapping up ornaments and things."

Glen nodded. "I suppose so. But why didn't we notice it before? And how did it catch on fire?"

No one answered. Jess had crouched down and was peering at the floor where the fire had been. They'd soaked it pretty thoroughly, but beyond the wet area there were some small splodgy and sooty marks going across the hall carpet. In the gloom it was hard to make out what they were.

Then Emma said, "Hey, what's this?"

She was prodding at something in the soggy heap. Glen went to look, and picked the object up, shaking water from it.

"What the heck. . .?" he said softly.

It was a candle. Or rather, the stub of a candle: most of it had been burned away. Jess stared at it, and suddenly felt as if icy spiders were crawling over her skin.

"Glen. . ." she said in a peculiar voice. "Have you got a torch anywhere?"

"There's one in the kitchen, I think," Glen replied. "Why? What do—" He saw her face. "Jess?"

"Just get the torch," said Jess unsteadily.

He did. Jess switched it on. She looked at the sooty marks on the floor again. And she felt sick.

"They look like pawprints," she whispered.

"Pawprints?" Jamie came to peer. "No way. They're just round blobs; an animal's prints are—"

"I don't mean an animal," Jess interrupted. "They make me think of . . . *Bear*."

It was such a crazy thing to say that she expected the others to start laughing. But they didn't. Instead they stared at her, and no one spoke for what seemed a very long time. Then: "No," said Emma. "It can't be. . ."

"You put him on the bonfire, Jess," Jamie added. He looked a bit pale. "You did – didn't you?"

"Yes," Jess whispered.

"And you saw your neighbour light it."

"Yes."

"So Bear's gone. We *know* he has."

"Yes," Jess whispered for the third time. "Unless. . ."

"Unless what?" Emma demanded sharply. But before Jess could answer, Glen cut in.

"I know what Jess is thinking. If Bear can move around on his own – and we know he can – then he might have escaped before the fire was lit."

Jamie turned to Jess again. "But you tied him up! You told us!"

Jess nodded miserably. Yes, she'd tied Bear up, and put a bandage over his eyes. She'd done everything she could to make sure he wouldn't get away. But it had been dawn when she'd hidden Bear in the pile of wood and garden rubbish. Bonfire Bill hadn't actually lit the fire for several more hours.

Was it possible that Bear had got away? She had a hideous feeling that it was. But instead of returning to Jess's house, he'd made his way back to his old home, where he'd caused havoc and misery for so many years.

"I think," she said, "we'd better see if we can find anything."

Glen shone the torch along the line of splodgy prints again, and they saw that the marks led across the hall to a door under the staircase.

"What's that?" Emma asked softly. "A cupboard?"

Glen shook his head. "No such luck. It's the door to the cellar."

Jess's heart started to sink. "Is there anything down there?" she said.

"I don't know," Glen replied. "I don't think Dad's even looked yet."

Her heart crashed into her shoes. The idea of hunting for Bear in a dark, dank underground room was more than creepy – it was *frightening*. Even if the cellar was only half as cluttered as the attic, there would be hundreds of hiding places. Another awful possibility occurred to her then, and she said, "Is that the only way in and out?"

"I don't know," Glen said again. "You mean, if there's another door, Bear might sneak out again?"

"Yeah." Jess licked her lips nervously. "But if there isn't another door, and we all go down there, he could double back and. . ." She nodded, towards the burned papers. She didn't need to say the rest.

Emma looked horrified. "We'd be trapped!"

"Yeah," Glen agreed. "We would. OK, so one of us had better stay up here and keep watch while the others go down to the cellar."

"Can it be me?" Emma begged. "Please! I'm too scared. There might be creepy-crawlies, and I hate them!"

It was pretty dumb to be scared of creepy-crawlies when there was Bear to worry about, Jess thought. But the last thing they needed was someone having hysterics all over the place, so she said, "All right, then. But if you see anything suspicious, just yell!"

"I will!"

109

The cellar door, they found, was slightly ajar, which gave their nerves an extra twinge. With Glen leading the way and shining the torch, they went slowly and carefully down the steep stairs. The pawprints continued for four or five steps then faded out as the soot wore off Bear's feet. But it was enough to tell them that he had come this way.

The cellar was huge – and unpleasantly dark. There was a narrow window, but it was set high up in the wall, and it was so grimy that it turned the daylight a sickly green. The bottom of it was on a level with the garden, and when Glen tried the catch it was rusted solid.

"We'll never shift this," he said.

"Well, if we can't, neither can Bear," Jess pointed out. "So he can't possibly have gone this way."

"Right. Which means he's got to be in here." Glen took a deep breath. "Do your stuff with the torch, Jess, and we'll get hunting."

By the torchlight they saw that the cellar wasn't full of junk like the attics, but there was still enough stuff down there – tools, bits of wood, old rolls of carpet – to make them stare around in dismay.

"He could be anywhere," Jamie whispered.

Glen had been thinking, and had a plan. "If you and I start shifting this stuff, and Jess stands in the middle with the torch, that's our best chance of spotting him if he tries to sneak away."

"OK," said Jess. She took the torch and swung it slowly from side to side as Glen and Jamie began their search. She felt very nervous, and had to keep fighting an awful urge to look over her shoulder. In the end she backed right up against the wall. That way, if anything was there, it couldn't creep up behind her.

Shadows jumped and flickered as the torch beam swung, but there was no sign of a little shape scurrying furtively away. Jess's heart was thumping as she watched Glen and Jamie moving boards and boxes and a battered old chest of drawers. They disturbed several enormous spiders, which scuttled across the floor and made her shudder, but by the time they'd shifted everything there was to shift, they'd found no sign of Bear.

"He's *got* to be down here somewhere!" Jamie said. "He couldn't possibly have opened the window, and there's no other way out!"

Jess glanced nervously up at the cobwebby ceiling, half expecting to see Bear hanging upside-down by his feet and leering at them.

"Come on," said Glen wearily. "Let's go through this stuff again. We must have missed something."

"We ought to check on Emma," Jess said. "You know how twitchy she is; if we leave her alone for too long she'll get the wind up." The truth was, she was twitchy too. She wanted an excuse to get out of the cellar, even if it was only for a minute. So she was just about to add, "I'll go, shall I?" when it happened.

For one shocking moment they didn't know what the shrill noise from overhead was. But then they realized.

It was Emma. She was screaming as if she was being murdered.

12

"It was *him*!" Emma babbled hysterically. "He was here, he was right *here*!"

Glen grabbed her shoulders. "Where did he go?"

Emma waved wildly towards the kitchen, and the two boys ran in pursuit. Against a background of distant banging and crashing, Jess struggled to calm her friend down and find out what had happened.

"I only looked away for a moment," Emma sobbed. "Then suddenly I felt this pain, and I jumped, and – and – oh, it was *horrible*!"

"Pain?" Jess echoed. "Where?"

"In my leg! There – look!"

Emma hopped on one foot. Jess looked – and her eyes widened.

Jamie and Glen came back then. "Nothing," Jamie said. "He's vanished." He stared hard at Emma. "If he was ever there at all."

"He was," said Jess grimly. "And he did *that*."

She pointed to a mark on Emma's bare leg, just above her ankle. It was a burn mark.

Jamie turned pale. "Oh, God!" He glanced at Glen. "What we found – d'you think. . . ?"

"Yeah," said Glen. "I think." He held out his hand. "This was on the kitchen floor."

He dropped a used match into Jess's palm.

Suddenly none of them wanted to be inside the house, so they took Emma out to the garden and got the rest of the story from her. It had been Bear, all right. Emma had been looking around the hall, not at the cellar stairs, when there was a sudden scuffling noise near her feet, a flicker of light, and an instant later she'd felt the searing pain in her leg. She'd seen Bear as he scurried away towards the kitchen. He was going on all fours, like a real animal. And he was moving fast.

"I didn't want to believe what Jess told us," Emma said, her voice still jittery. "But after this. . ."

"What I want to know," said Glen ominously, "is, where's Bear gone now?"

"If he can run as fast as Emma says, he could be anywhere." Jamie stared back at the house, which looked secretive and sinister. "In there, in the garden—"

"Don't!" Emma pleaded, shuddering. "I'm not going back in that house. My leg hurts, and I'm scared, and I want to go home!"

"But what are we going to do about Bear?" Jess protested.

"Emma ought to get that burn seen to," said Jamie. "Anyway, I reckon Bear'll stay around here. This is his home, after all. And the further we are away from him, the happier I'll be!"

Emma agreed, and nothing Jess could say would change her mind. She was going home, and that was that. And Jamie said he was going with her.

"Look," he reasoned. "If we leave Bear here, and don't disturb him, then our bad luck might stop. It's worth a try, anyway. If we go looking for him, we could only end up making everything worse."

He might be right, Jess thought. She wanted to believe him, because it was an answer to all their troubles. "Well. . ." she began uncertainly.

"Come on!" Emma urged. She was already heading for the front gate. "I'm not hanging around here any more, so if you don't hurry up, I'll go without you."

"All right!" Then Jess looked uncertainly at Glen. "What about you?"

Glen shrugged. "Oh . . . I'll go home too, I suppose." He looked back at the house, and Jess wondered if he had something else in mind. But he didn't say so, and Emma was calling "Come on!" again, so she only said, "Look, you ring us or we'll ring you, OK? Later – or tomorrow. And if anything happens. . ."

"OK." Glen shrugged. "See you, then. 'Bye!"

Jess looked back as she went down the street with Emma and Jamie. Glen was still standing in the garden, with his hands deep in his pockets. He was staring at the ground and he didn't glance up at her. *Was* he going home? Yes, of course he was. He'd just lock the house up, then he'd be off. He wouldn't stay around. He had more sense. Didn't he?

She pushed the doubt away, and hurried after her friends.

Jess left Emma and Jamie at the town bus stop. She didn't enjoy the walk home at all, firstly because the day was getting hotter and she felt sweaty and uncomfortable, and secondly because she kept getting nasty little reminders of Bear and what he'd tried to do.

She heard the siren wailing half a minute before the two fire engines came screeching down the road and hurtled past her with their blue lights flashing. For a horrible moment Jess wondered if the fire was at Aunt Lucy's house, but then she worked out that the engines were going in the wrong direction. It was a relief, but it shook her all the same.

Further on there was a billboard at the side of the road. This morning when she passed, two men had been tearing down the old poster, and now a new one had been put up. It was all about fire safety. Jess stopped, staring at it. It was only a coincidence – of course it was – but it gave her the creeps.

Then, last and worst of all, there was Bonfire Bill. Jess saw the smoke billowing from his garden as she turned the corner of her street. It was much thicker and darker than usual, and, alarmed, she ran round by the back way to see what was going on.

Bill was in his garden, and so were several other neighbours, including her mum. They were hosing water on to the remains of this morning's bonfire, and they all looked dishevelled and a bit shaken.

"I don't know how it happened," Bonfire Bill was saying apologetically as Jess came within earshot. "It was only smouldering a bit – the last embers, you know – then suddenly it flared up again!"

"Well, it just goes to show you can't be too careful, doesn't it?" Jess's mum replied sourly. "And if it means you won't have so many bonfires in the future, then we'll all be grateful! Right – it's properly out now, so I'm going indoors!"

Mum and Jess met at the back door, and Jess asked breathlessly, "What happened?"

"Silly old—" Mum bit back the word she was going to say. "He only went and let it get out of control, didn't he? Nearly set a tree and two bushes on fire, and if we hadn't gone to help him, half the street'd probably be ablaze by now!"

Mum was exaggerating, but none the less Jess felt an icy shiver go through her. The fire engines. The billboard. And now the next-door neighbour. Three things? It was starting to push coincidence a bit far.

"That man's a menace with his fires!" Mum went on as she slammed the back door. "And in this weather, too. Still, like I said, if it shakes him up then perhaps he won't have so many bonfires from now on."

Jess didn't speak. In fact she hadn't said anything at all since she'd asked what was going on. The more she thought about these "coincidences", the less she liked them. It looked as if Jamie had been wrong when he'd said that Bear's influence would fade now that he was back at Aunt Lucy's house and out of their way. What was the old proverb? "Out of sight, out of mind", that was it. *Ha!* Jess thought. Whoever wrote that one had never encountered anything like Bear.

She didn't feel like going out again, but went to her room and tried to find something to take her mind off her worries. The afternoon was really boiling hot now, which didn't help. There'd probably be a thunderstorm before long, and that would really put the lid on her mood.

She was playing a computer game when suddenly there was a horrified yell from below.

"Mum?" Jess jumped to her feet.

Then her nose caught the burning smell.

"*Mum!*" She pounded downstairs. The kitchen was full of smoke, and Mum was at the cooker. She'd thrown something over the top of it, and with a shock Jess recognized the fire blanket that was kept next to the extinguisher in the cupboard. Tendrils of smoke leaked from under it, and the stink of scorching oil made her eyes water.

"I must have turned the chip pan on by accident!" Mum said in a shaky voice. "I was standing by the sink and I heard a whoosh, and next thing I knew it was going up in flames!"

Luckily she'd acted fast, turning the cooker off and smothering the fire with the blanket.

There was no real damage, apart from some greasy scorching on the walls. But she was shaken – and so was Jess. This was the fourth coincidence. And four was too many.

Fire. It was Bear's favourite weapon. This morning Jess had tried to use it against him, but the plan hadn't worked and now he was *really* out for revenge. Jess was more scared than she'd ever been in her life. What could happen next? She tried to think of all the possible fire sources in the house, and the list was terrifying. The TV, the video, kitchen gadgets, her computer – anything electrical might short-circuit. Even more likely was the gas. You heard so many stories of gas mains blowing up. Then what about the car? She thought of the petrol tank, and felt sick with fright. There were so many potential dangers. And Bear was just waiting to strike again.

Mum was still in the kitchen, waiting for the chip pan to cool down so that she could put it outside and clean up. Jess went into the sitting-room and unplugged everything she could find. Never mind explaining – she'd sort that out later. Then she went back to her room and unplugged her computer and hi-fi. No way was she going to use either of them.

And then she wondered if Emma and Jamie were all right. . .

Emma answered the phone. She sounded jittery, but Jess assumed it was because of what had happened earlier. She was wrong.

"I was j-just going to call you," Emma stammered. "Oh, Jess, it's so *scary* – awful things keep happening! Our TV blew up, and the plug was sparking like crazy. Then I singed my hair when I tried to light the gas cooker. And someone threw a cigarette-end into our front garden as they walked past, and it wasn't out, and it nearly set the hedge on fire!" She swallowed. "And the worst thing is, I just phoned Jamie, and it's happening to him, too! Oh, Jess, what are we going to *do*?"

"I think we'd better ring Glen," said Jess. "This isn't going to stop unless we can get rid of Bear for good. So if he's still at Aunt Lucy's house, we're going to need Glen's help."

"I don't want to go back there!" Emma wailed.

"You'll have to! We all will. Look, I'll phone Glen now and ring you back, OK?"

Emma paused. Then, "OK," she said weakly. "But I still don't want—"

"Talk to you later," said Jess, and put the phone down.

Glen wasn't at home. His mum said he'd gone out early this morning and wasn't back yet; did Jess want her to give him a message when he came in? Jess said, "Oh – um – could you just tell him Jess rang? Thanks. 'Bye."

Her heart was thumping as she replaced the receiver. Where *was* Glen? Surely he couldn't still be at Aunt Lucy's house. He wasn't that stupid, was he? No, no – he must have gone into town or something. Right at this moment he was probably sitting in a burger bar, or the cinema, or messing around in the park. He wasn't at the house. Not on his own. He *couldn't* be.

Trying to tell herself that there was nothing to worry about, she called Emma back. Emma was convinced that Glen had stayed behind and Bear had "got" him. But Jess reminded her that Glen had never touched Bear, so he wasn't infected with the jinx.

"It's *us* he's after, not Glen," she said

sombrely. "We'll have to hang on till he gets home. And while we're waiting, we'd just better be careful!"

How many times have we said that to each other in the last few days? Jess wondered as she hung up. She thought about ringing Jamie but decided there was no point. At least nothing *really* bad had happened yet, so maybe they had a bit of time.

But not much time. She was as sure of that as she'd ever been of anything. Not much time at all.

By half-past four there hadn't been any more accidents, and Jess was getting worried. The situation was too quiet; she didn't trust it. And where was Glen? He hadn't phoned back yet. She needed to talk to him.

At last, at a quarter to five, she couldn't stand the waiting any longer. She went to the phone, and was just about to pick it up and dial Glen's number again when it rang, making her jump.

She grabbed the receiver and almost shouted, "Hello?"

"Jess – it's me!" It was Glen's voice, and Jess

felt a huge surge of relief. But the relief didn't last long.

"I'm in a call-box near Aunt Lucy's," Glen went on. "Look – can you ring the others? I think you'd all better get over here – and *fast*!"

13

It was hotter than ever now. Jess was perspiring as she turned into Aunt Lucy's road, and the air was stifling, as if there wasn't enough left for breathing. All the same, she had run most of the way. Glen hadn't explained much on the phone, but the urgent tone of his voice had been enough to alarm her.

Emma and Jamie wouldn't be here yet. Jess just hoped that they wouldn't chicken out. They'd promised to come, but Emma in particular had been very unwilling, especially as Jess couldn't tell her what was going on. Well, she'd find that out soon enough. Glen should be waiting for her in the garden.

He was, and as the gate clicked he appeared from the overgrown shrubbery.

"Am I glad to see you!" he said with relief. "Did you ring the others? Are they coming?"

"Yes, and I hope so," said Jess. "What's going on? You sounded really weird on the phone."

"Yeah, well, you'll see why in a minute. Come on."

He turned towards the house, and Jess's pulse raced. "In there?"

Glen nodded. "Sorry. If you want to wait for Emma and Jamie. . ."

"No." She swallowed. "No, it's OK. I'm coming."

The sun had vanished and there was a thick, yellowish haze in the sky now. Inside the house it was gloomier than ever – and over everything hung a weird, sickly-flowery smell that puzzled Jess.

Heading for the stairs, Glen was saying, "It's in the attic. I'd have brought it down if I could, but—"

"Glen. . ." Emma stopped dead in the hall. "What's all *this*?"

There were patches of what looked like white powder all over the floor. Most of it seemed to be concentrated around the doors; in fact she'd trodden in some as she came in.

"Oh, that." Glen had stopped too. "It's flour. Well, mostly. I put it there."

Jess was completely baffled. "Whatever for?"

Glen explained. Bear could be anywhere in the house, and he was so small that he could hide in hundreds of different nooks and crannies. He could easily sneak up on them, as he'd done with Emma, and they'd never even know he was lurking. What they needed was a way to keep track of him. So Glen had had the idea of sprinkling flour in front of all the doors and windows in the house. That way, Bear wouldn't be able to go very far without leaving footprints.

"It's not perfect," Glen said, "but if he moves around, at least we'll have some idea where he goes." He grinned sheepishly at Jess. "I used all sorts of things: flour, cleaning powder – even some talc I found upstairs. That's why it pongs a bit. Mildew and Luxurious Lavender don't really mix."

"I think it's a brill idea," said Jess. "Makes me feel safer. I mean, it's bad enough him doing things at a distance, but. . ." Glen looked puzzled, and she paused. "Ah – of course. You don't know, do you? About the things that've been happening to me and the others."

Glen didn't, and when she told him, he was horrified. "Oh, hell!" he said. "And we all thought you were going to be safer once you were away from here!"

Jess hadn't thought that, but she didn't comment. All she said was, "Have you found any prints yet?"

"No. Bear probably saw me putting the flour down, and he's worked out what it's for. So he's lying low till he works out a way to get round it." Glen scuffed the floor with one foot. "Still, if it keeps him in one place for a bit, that's got to be a good thing."

Jess looked around at the unmarked white patches and hoped he was right. "OK," she said. "Then let's get up to the attic, while he's still quiet."

* * *

"I meant to go home after you'd gone," Glen told her as they climbed the stairs. "But then I had the idea about the flour, and when I'd done that I thought I'd hang around to see if Bear fell for it. That was pretty boring, so I came back up here and started going through that junk again. That was when I found it."

They went into the attic, carefully stepping over the flour around the door. Glen had been shoving some of the larger objects around and it was more of a mess than ever. Jess stared at it in dismay, but he beckoned her towards the far end of the room, where a big chest of drawers was wedged between a crammed bookcase and a stack of heavy picture frames.

The bottom drawer of the chest wasn't shut properly, and some pieces of paper and card were sticking out. Some more pieces lay on top of the chest, and Glen handed two of them to Jess.

"The drawer's jammed and I can't get it open," he said. "But I managed to pull these out."

There was a letter, and a greetings card with a picture of butterflies on it. Jess opened the card. It was written with an old-fashioned pen and it said: "*To dear little Lucy on her special day. Wishing you many happy returns, from Cousin Grace.*"

Jess looked blankly at Glen. "So what?" she asked.

"Read the letter," said Glen.

The letter, too, was from "Cousin Grace" to "dear little Lucy". It started off by wishing her many happy returns again – but underneath there was something else. Something that chilled Jess's blood.

"*For your present on your eighth birthday, I give you my own little Bear. You are a good child, and so I know you will take great care of him and treat him kindly. You must always be kind to him, for my sake. I send you my love and good wishes, dear; from Cousin Grace.*"

The colour drained from Jess's face. "It's Bear," she hissed. "It's *got* to be!"

"Too right," said Glen. "And there's more." He picked up the other papers. "I'd never heard of Cousin Grace. But then I looked at this."

It was another card, with a black border, and

on the front were the words, "*With deepest sympathy*". Someone had died . . . and Jess guessed even before she opened it who that someone was.

She was right. The card was from a family called Parker, and the sorrowful message was all about "Poor Grace", who had apparently been "taken so suddenly". It was dated November 1920. Jess did some rapid mental maths. Aunt Lucy had been getting on for ninety when she died. Which meant she must have been born just after 1910. So by 1920, she'd have been about. . .

Eight.

"Oh, God!" Jess whispered.

Glen nodded grimly. "Bear belonged to Cousin Grace, and she gave him to Aunt Lucy, and then she died – suddenly – pretty soon afterwards. It all adds up, doesn't it?"

"She must have thought she could get rid of the jinx by giving Bear away," said Jess. "But to pass him on to a little kid – that's *disgusting*!"

Glen shrugged. "Maybe she was desperate, or mad, or both. Anyway, it didn't do her much good, did it?" He turned to the chest of drawers. "The thing is, we've got some information about Bear. I'll bet anything that there's more in there, and it could be exactly what we need. I can't get the drawer open any further, but maybe two of us could do it."

"Right!" said Jess. "Then for starters, let's pull it out a bit further and make it easier to get at."

They grabbed the chest between them and started to heave. With an almighty scraping noise they dragged it a few centimetres forward – and then, so fast that it was almost a blur, something shot out from behind it. A small brown shape, scuttling across the floor. . .

Jess screamed, "*It's him! Oh, quick – stop him!*"

Glen didn't pause to think. He made a flying leap, like a rugby tackle, and as he crashed to the floor his hands clamped tightly round Bear. Jess heard a loud squeak, like ordinary teddy-bears make when you press their stomachs. Then Glen yelled in pain and rolled over, clutching his fingers.

"He *bit* me! Oww!"

Bear hurtled out of the door.

Jess didn't dither. She pelted after Bear, who was scrabbling, fast, down the attic stairs. He saw her coming and dived for the gap between two banisters. Jess made a despairing grab, but she was too late. Bear wriggled through the gap, and jumped. He hit the floor below, bounced, regained his balance – and vanished at top speed along the landing.

Jess whirled back to the attic. Glen was getting to his feet, still nursing his hand. To her horror, Jess saw that his fingertips had beads of blood on them.

"He's got *teeth*!" Glen said in a shocked voice.

By now, Jess was ready to believe anything about Bear. She told him what had happened, adding, "He could be anywhere. We'll never find him."

"Don't forget the flour," said Glen. "He'll leave a trail. Look, let's finish shifting that chest of drawers, then we'll track him and see where he went."

Jess didn't like leaving Bear to prowl freely around the house, but she couldn't see any alternative. They hauled the chest far enough out to get at it properly, then wrestled with the jammed drawer. It came free at last, jerking open with a wallop that sent them both staggering back, and a fat wad of papers spilled out.

"Wow!" Glen stared at them. "There's tonnes of stuff here – it'll take ages to go through it all!"

"Tell you what," said Jess, "you get started, and I'll find out where Bear's gone. I'll feel a lot happier once we know where he is."

Glen agreed, so Jess left him to it. But by the time she reached the landing she was beginning to wish she hadn't offered to go on her own. The thought that Bear might be lurking somewhere nearby was giving her nerves a bad time, and she almost ran back to the attic to ask Glen if he'd come with her. Only the fact that she didn't want to look like a gutless prat stopped her, and she made herself go on.

There were pawprints in the flour patch at the end of the landing, showing that Bear had gone down to the ground floor. Jess followed, and found more prints leading to the kitchen. So far, so good. From there, Bear either had to get out to the garden – in which case he'd be well out of the way – or double back. As there was only one set of prints, he obviously hadn't done that yet. So if she shut the kitchen door. . .

Jess quietly eased it closed, and breathed a sigh of relief. She was about to head for the stairs again when there was a bang on the front door, and a voice called, "Hello? Anyone there?"

It was Jamie, and Emma was with him.

"Am I glad to see you two!" Jess said as they came in. "Glen's found something. He's up in the attic – come on."

Emma hung back. "I'm not supposed to stay long," she muttered. "Mum says I've got to be home by half-past seven, and it's already gone six."

"Well, you'd better get a move on then, hadn't you?" Jess retorted unsympathetically. She wasn't in the mood for Emma's scaredy-cat dithering.

"We'd better all go soon, if we don't want to get wet," said Jamie as they started up the stairs. "Have you seen the sky? There's going to be an absolutely *mega* storm!"

Emma hadn't looked, but now he'd said it she realized that the light was a lot gloomier than it should have been, even this late in the day. She peered through the landing window as they passed, and Jamie was dead right. The sun had completely vanished and the sky was an ominous sulphur colour.

"OK," she said, "then we won't hang around. We'll see how Glen's getting on, and we'll tell you everything that's happened, then we'll get out of here. Glen!" She raised her voice. "Bear's hiding in the kitchen, and I've shut the door on him, and Jamie and Em have come!"

"Great!" came the reply. "And I've found some more stuff."

Jess was surprised to see that the attic door was closed. It must have swung back when she left, and she reached out to open it.

It wouldn't open.

"Glen?" She rattled the handle. "Glen! Have you locked the door?"

"Course not!"

"Well, it won't open. It's stuck."

"Uh?" They heard footsteps, then the handle was rattled again from the other side. "What the heck. . ." said Glen. Then, with fear creeping into his voice, he added: "Jess, it isn't stuck. It's *locked*!"

14

"How did he *do* it?" Jess said, watching Jamie waggle a piece of wire in the lock. "He was downstairs, I *know* he was!"

"He must have doubled back when you weren't looking," Jamie said through clenched teeth. "'Cos he's the only one who could possibly have locked Glen in. Oh, this is *useless*! We're going to have to bust the lock!"

"Well, hurry up and do it, then!" Emma urged. "I'm scared, and I want—"

"To go home, we know!" Jess interrupted. "Stop whingeing about it and do something useful!"

"Yeah," Jamie added. "Go to the cellar and see if you can find a hammer and chisel."

Emma looked horrified. "I'm not going down there on my own!"

Jess rolled her eyes heavenwards. "All right, I'll come with you." Then a thought struck her. "Hey – there's one thing we haven't thought of." She put her mouth close to the door. "Glen! What about a key? There must be one somewhere."

"Yeah," came Glen's voice. "There's a whole load of keys hanging on a board in the big kitchen cupboard. Only Bear's got this one, hasn't he?"

"Oh. Yeah, right; of course. Come on then, Em; let's find a hammer."

She went back downstairs, towing the reluctant Emma with her. The sky was so heavy now that they needed a torch to see where they were going. Jess found Glen's in the kitchen, and they headed for the cellar door.

As Jess opened it, a colossal flash lit up the house. Emma screamed, and her scream was drowned by a crash of thunder that seemed to shake the walls.

"Je-ess!" Emma shut her eyes and covered her ears.

Jess was shaken, too, but she didn't want to admit it. "Oh, shut up!" she snapped. "It's only thunder. You've never been frightened of it before."

"But this is *different!*" Emma whined.

"No, it isn't. Come on, and stop being such a wimp!"

Emma insisted on carrying the torch, and they went carefully down the cellar stairs. What with the storm and the overgrown garden, the high, narrow window hardly let in any light at all, and as Emma flashed the torch around, Jess looked for a likely place for someone to keep a hammer. Ah – that bench had some tools on it. She found what she wanted and they turned to go. The torch beam swung round. . .

And fell like a spotlight on Bear.

He was half-way across the floor, heading towards them. As the light caught him, he froze, then his eyes flashed in a ferocious glare, and a weird sound that was half squeak and half snarl came from his throat.

Emma shrieked like a banshee and dropped

the torch. Jess heard it break and the batteries fall out, and the cellar was plunged into darkness.

"*No!*" Emma screamed. "*Oh, Je-e-ess!*"

"You prat!" Jess yelled. She couldn't see a thing, and panic surged inside her. *Where was Bear?* He could be creeping up on them, getting ready to—

Then a second enormous flash of lightning lit up the cellar, enough for Jess to see Bear again. He was scuttling across the floor, in the direction of the stairs, and with an awful jolt Jess realized what he meant to do.

"*Em! Quick!*" She flung herself towards the staircase. Scrambling up in the gloom, she tripped and sprawled, grazing her hands and shins. As she picked herself up, a noise rang out that struck terror into her.

The noise of the door above her slamming.

"Oh, no!" Jess scrabbled to the top of the stairs and grabbed the door handle, twisting and pulling. It wouldn't budge. Something with far more strength than she had was gripping it from the other side.

"No!" Jess yelled again. "Open it! Let me out!"

She thumped the door with both fists, but the only reply she got was a firm *click* as a key was turned in the lock.

"Jess?" Emma called quaveringly from below. "What's going on?"

"Bear's gone," said Jess unsteadily. "And he's locked us in." Shoulders slumping, she went back to the cellar. She could just make out Emma's shape in the gloom. Emma was shaking, and biting her knuckles. "What are we going to do?" she whimpered.

Glen locked in the attic. Herself and Emma locked in the cellar. That just left Jamie. How long before he worked out that something was wrong, and came looking for them? Five minutes? Ten? And when he did, would Bear have a trap waiting for him, too?

"Emma!" Jess grabbed her friend by the shoulders and shook her. "We've got to warn Jamie! If Bear manages to lock him in somewhere, too—"

"Oh, God!" Emma gasped. "Then he'll have trapped all four of us! He can do absolutely *anything*, and we won't be able to stop him!"

"Right! Look, you go to the door and start thumping and yelling, and I'm going to try and open that window and shout through it!"

Emma nodded and ran up the stairs, and Jess dragged a box under the cellar window. Lightning flared twice more as she climbed on to the box, and this time the thunder was only a couple of seconds behind. The storm must be almost on top of them.

The catch was so solidly rusted that it would have taken Rambo to shift it. Jess didn't even bother to try. Snatching the hammer and turning her head away, she smashed the glass. The noise of it breaking was drowned by another bawl of thunder, and rain came teeming in. There was a real downpour out there – if Jamie was still at the top of the house, he'd never hear her shouting over that noise!

All the same she tried, yelling the boys' names with all the strength she could find. No one answered, and in this weather there was no one in the street, either. Jess was getting hoarse when suddenly Emma came pelting back.

"Jess!" Another lightning flash showed Emma's face stark and terrified. "In the hall – I can smell smoke!"

"*What?*" Jess almost fell off the box, and

they both ran back up the stairs. There was smoke, all right. Jess couldn't just smell it, she could *see* it starting to seep in under the door.

Bear had lit another fire.

"We'll be burned to death!" Emma howled. "Oh, Jess!"

The broken window – was it big enough to squeeze through? Jess hadn't thought so or she'd have tried before. But this was a real emergency.

She whirled round and raced back, with Emma at her heels. Emma saw at once what she meant to do, and she said, "It's too small, you'll never get through it!"

"I've got to try!" Jess checked that there was no glass left to cut her, and pushed her head through the gap. Then her shoulders. So far, so good. Lightning flashed again, making her flinch, and the rain poured over her face and hair. She spluttered it away. Arms first – that was it. Now she could grab hold of a bush to lever herself up.

Then suddenly she was stuck. She kicked and wriggled, but nothing happened, and frantically she shouted to Emma, "Give me a shove!"

Emma shoved, putting all her strength into it. For several dreadful moments Jess thought it wasn't going to work. Then she felt something give, and suddenly, like a cork popping out of a bottle, she fell out into the garden.

The biggest lightning flash yet greeted her as she rolled over and jumped to her feet. Over the din of the thunder she called, "Give me the hammer and chisel, *quick*!"

Emma hurled them through. "Hurry, Jess, hurry!" she pleaded, but Jess was already racing round the side of the house. The back door wasn't locked and she charged into the kitchen. A whirl of smoke met her in the hall, and she saw the pile of papers and old leaves smouldering in the middle of the floor.

"*Jamie!*" she bawled up the stairs. "Get down here, *fast*!"

Feet pounded as Jess dropped her tools and raced back to the kitchen for a bowl, a bucket – anything that would hold water. She was flinging the first lot on to the fire when Jamie appeared. Luckily, the pile had been damp to start with and there weren't any flames. Between them they put it out in minutes, then stood coughing and wiping their smoke-stained faces with even grimier hands.

"Bear?" Jamie panted.

Jess nodded. "Bear. He locked us in the cellar. I got out through the window, but Em's still in there. We'd better—" She stopped, tensing. "What was that?"

"What?"

"I don't know – a sort of crackling. It came from upstairs. . ."

Jamie ran to the foot of the stairs and peered up. "There's some sort of light flickering." His eyes widened. "Oh, my God! *He's started another fire!*"

This time he'd set light to the cloth that covered a small table on the landing. Jamie smothered the cloth in curtains and hurled the whole bundle out of the window. As it fell, hissing and sputtering in the pouring rain, Jess heard a rattling noise behind them. She whirled, and was just in time to see Bear bouncing down the attic stairs. He saw her and leered at her – she heard that ugly half-squeak, half-snarl again – then he skidded round the corner and vanished. He was scurrying on two legs now, fast as a rat, and horror hit Jess as she realized what he'd been carrying: a bunch of keys in one paw and a box of matches in the other.

With a hideous shock she saw Bear's scheme. The big fire he'd tried to start in the hall hadn't worked, so instead he was going to start little ones all over the house – so many that she and the others wouldn't be able to put them all out.

"*Jamie!*" She ran to him and gasped out what Bear planned to do. "Emma and Glen are still trapped! We've got to get them out!"

"Those tools—"

"They're in the hall!"

They pounded downstairs and Jamie grabbed the hammer and chisel. "Glen first," he said. "He's in more danger. I'll do it – you stay here in case Bear comes back this way!"

Emma's voice quavered from behind the cellar door. "What's going on? What are you doing?"

"It's all right – back in a sec!" Jess didn't wait to say any more but ran back to the kitchen as Jamie took the stairs two at a time. She wanted to fill every bucket and bowl she could find, and take something heavy to use as a weapon. Just in case.

Her heart was going like a hammer under her ribs as she came back with a rolling pin in one hand and a full bucket of water in the other. The lightning outside was almost continuous now, and between thunderclaps the sounds of bashing and hammering came from the top of the house. *Oh, hurry, Jamie, hurry!* Jess prayed. Where was Bear now? Where would he start the next fire? The patches of flour were no use any more; they'd trampled them so much that Bear could have done a dance on them and it wouldn't have shown.

Then from the landing a new light flared.

And over the banisters, what looked like a ball of fire plummeted towards her.

15

Jess screamed, leaping clear just in time as the burning bedspread hit the hall floor. She hurled the contents of the bucket over it, but her aim was panicky and half the water was wasted. The flames hissed, then flared up again.

"*Jamie!*" Jess screeched.

Bash – bang – CRASH! came from upstairs, then the noise of two pairs of running feet. Jamie had done it – he'd broken down the attic door! He and Glen appeared as Jess was struggling back from the kitchen with two more loads of water. Emma was yelling from behind the door now, and Jamie shouted, "He's started two more fires upstairs! We can't stop him; we've just got to get *out!*"

As he and Jess threw water on to the bed-spread, Glen called through the cellar door, "Emma! Can you get out through the window?"

"It's too small!" Jess said desperately. "I'm thinner than her, and I only just made it!"

"She'll have to try – it'll take too long to bust this door down! Quick! Bring the tools, and we'll help from outside!"

"But the house—" Jess began.

"Never mind the house! With any luck it'll burn to the ground, with Bear inside it!"

For a moment Jess felt a pang of awful guilt. *This is all my fault*, she thought. *If I hadn't got Glen involved in this. . .*

But that was crazy, wasn't it? It wasn't her fault at all. Whatever happened, even if Aunt Lucy's house *did* burn to the ground, there was only one person – or *thing* – to blame.

She shoved the thought aside and shouted to Emma, "*Em!* We're going round the outside – meet us by the window!"

The boys were already piling out of the front door, and she ran after them. As they emerged into the garden there was an enormous flash, and a split second later thunder exploded. Everyone flinched, and Glen said, "Who's got the guts to run to the phone box and call the fire brigade?"

Jamie volunteered, and raced away, hunching in the rain, as Jess and Glen hurried round to the cellar.

Emma was waiting. She'd climbed on to the box Jess had used, and her head was sticking out of the window. Rain streamed from her hair and face, mingling with tears of fright.

"I can't get through!" she sobbed. "I've tried, but it's no use!"

"OK." Glen looked at the window frame. "If I knock this out, it'll give us a few more centimetres. Stand well back, Emma."

Emma scrambled down, and Glen swung the hammer. The wooden frame was already half rotten, and it only took four blows before the whole thing fell out.

"Try now, Em!" Jess urged.

Emma tried. "I can't! No, wait a minute. . ."

"Grab her arms!" shouted Glen. "Pull!"

"Ahh!" Emma groaned. "Oooo – *oof!*"

One final heave sent Jess and Glen tumbling

backwards as Emma came out through the hole. Not just wet now but muddy too from the earth, they all ducked as another enormous lightning flash seared across the sky.

"This storm's getting worse!" Glen bawled over the thunder. "It must be right overhead now!"

The girls didn't bother to answer him. They were too busy getting to their feet and brushing off the worst of the wet earth. Jess stood upright – and as she did so, she saw something out of the corner of her eye.

"What's that?" She snatched at Glen's arm, pointing into the overgrown bushes. Something was moving there – something small, scurrying furtively. A cat? No way, not in this weather! It had to be. . .

Jess yelled, *"Bear!"* and flung herself towards the bush. There was a scrabble and a flurry and the horrible squeak-snarl noise she'd heard before, then her hands clamped on something soft and squodgy, that wriggled like mad in her grip.

"I've got him, I've got him!" Jess backed out of the bush, and Emma's eyes bulged in horror.

"Jess, *no*! Put him down – he's *dangerous*!"

Bear squeak-snarled again, his beady little eyes glaring like fire at Jess. He wasn't pretending to be a toy any more. He opened his mouth, showing rows of tiny, vicious teeth. Then he twisted his head round, lungeing. . .

"*No you don't!*" Jess screamed. She gripped Bear's head to stop him biting, and suddenly felt a surge of raging fury. *So he thinks he can jinx us for ever, does he? I'll show you, Bear – I'll show you!* What was it Glen had said about the house burning down with Bear inside it? Bear had other ideas. He'd been trying to get away, and if he succeeded, he'd be back to haunt them again, wouldn't he? They'd never be free of him. Not unless he was *destroyed*.

Clutching Bear even more tightly, Jess started to walk towards the house.

"Jess, what are you doing?" Emma cried. "Come back!"

There was blazing light in all the ground-floor windows of the house as the fires inside took hold. Glen shouted, "Jess, it's dangerous!" but Jess ignored him. Bear was wriggling wildly now, but nothing on earth could have made

153

Jess let go. As if in a trance, she moved towards the front door. . .

"*Jess, you mustn't open it! The fire—*" But before Emma could scream the rest of her warning, Glen launched himself after Jess. He seized her and dragged her back, Jess yelling in protest and fighting him.

Then, without any warning at all—

BANG!!! It was as if a bomb had gone off. But it wasn't a bomb. The thunderbolt sheared down out of the clouds, and the whole world seemed to turn a shuddering blue as it hit the house roof. Every window blew out, and Jess, Emma and Glen were sent staggering backwards to the rickety garden fence, stunned and dazzled and deafened. They collapsed together in a tangle of arms and legs, and as the ground stopped shaking, flames roared up from the house's top floor.

"We've got to get out of here!" Glen yelled. "Next-door's garden – *move!*"

He and Emma started to scramble over the fence, breaking down more of it in their rush. Jess was about to follow when she realized that, incredibly, she was still holding Bear. She couldn't get any nearer to the house, but some broken pieces of wood from the fence were lying at her feet. . .

Jess played baseball at school, and she was good. She looked at Bear. Bear glared back. Jess smiled ferociously through her soaking hair, and picked up one of the pieces of wood.

She threw Bear as high as she could. And as he came down, she swung the wood like a baseball bat, and hit him with all her strength.

They all heard the thin, wailing squeal as Bear flew through the air. Legs flailing, he hurtled towards the house – and sailed through the gaping hole where the big bay window had been.

Straight into the heart of the fire.

Jess, Emma and Glen stood hypnotized, staring at the spot where Bear had disappeared. Jess heard – or maybe she imagined? – a last long, squeaking wail. Then for a moment there was only the sound of the pelting rain.

Until the howl of a siren shattered the quiet.

The fire engine skidded to a halt in the street and the firefighters came running. As the big hoses were rolled out, one firefighter crashed through the garden tangle to Jess and her friends.

"Come on, kids, let's get you away from here!"

High-pressure jets of water were smacking into the blazing house as he shepherded them away. People had come out of their houses to see what was going on, and there was quite a crowd in the street. Jess and the others joined Jamie, and all four stood in the pouring rain, watching as the firefighters did their work. After a while the fireman who'd led them to safety came over again. "Time you four were taken home!" he said kindly. "We're getting it under control now, so there's nothing to be scared of. Don't worry – everything's going to be OK!"

Jess looked at the house, then at the fireman. "Yeah," she said. "Thanks." *Everything's going to be OK*. He didn't know how right he was!

Emma said in a small voice, "My mum's going to kill me for being so late."

"Yeah," said Jess. "Mine, too. *And* I'm going to have to think of a way to explain what happened to Bear." One thing was for sure; Mum would *never* believe the truth. Then suddenly, though she didn't know why and it was completely stupid, she started to grin.